SPEAK, COMMENTARY

SPEAK, COMMENTARY

The Big Little Book of Fake
DVD Commentaries,
Wherein Well-Known Pundits
Make Impassioned Remarks About
Classic Science-Fiction Films
It's a Gas!

BY

JEFF ALEXANDER
&
TOM BISSELL

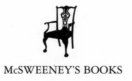

McSWEENEY'S BOOKS

McSWEENEY'S BOOKS
826 Valencia Street
San Francisco, CA 94110
429 Seventh Avenue
Brooklyn, NY 11215

www.mcsweeneys.net

To Ricardo Montalban and Charlton Heston

CONTENTS

INTRODUCTION, OR PREFACE 1

THE LORD OF THE RINGS: THE FELLOWSHIP OF THE RING 3
Platinum Series Special Extended Edition DVD
COMMENTARY BY HOWARD ZINN AND NOAM CHOMSKY

ALIENS 29
Special Red-State Edition DVD
COMMENTARY BY DINESH D'SOUZA AND ANN COULTER

STAR TREK II: THE WRATH OF KHAN 55
Trekker Mail-Order Edition DVD
COMMENTARY BY TERRY DWIBBLE AND STEVEN MCCRAY

PLANET OF THE APES 83
Limited-Edition 700 Club Gold Membership Bonus DVD
COMMENTARY BY JERRY FALWELL AND PAT ROBERTSON

STAR WARS: EPISODE I—THE PHANTOM MENACE 109
RNC Featured-Merchandise DVD
COMMENTARY BY DICK CHENEY AND WILLIAM BENNETT

INTRODUCTION,
OR PREFACE

IN THE BRIEF history of the DVD audio commentary, we have seen—or perhaps we should better say "heard"—a remarkable progression. We have gone from a film scholar observing the action on screen and dryly intoning observations along the lines of "Now observe the architectural integrity of this particular shot," to the film's director making a much more exciting and piquant and relevant observation, e.g., "Check this out, this is like, one of the most kick-ass shots in the whole fucking movie."

The question, then, is whether what we gain in terms of spontaneity and "insider" knowledge compensates for what we lose in terms of critical detachment, not to mention critical voice. It's not as if the studios have *entirely* given up on the two latters. For instance, in the spring of 1999, Paramount Home Video gathered a crew of distinguished critics, each of whom had at some point in his or her career been dubbed a "Paulette," into a recording facility on the Paramount lot and sat them around a Ouija board, the better to channel the spirit of Pauline Kael for an audio commentary to be used on the 25th Anniversary Edition DVD of Robert

Altman's *Nashville.* Things went very sluggishly, although the producers thought they detected a Kaelean intonation when one participant deemed an early scene "really terrific." Soon after that, though, it became clear that they couldn't properly channel Kael's spirit because Kael was not yet deceased.

(As for how things go when the participants in a given film, and its original critical adherents, are verifiably dead, well, just this morning I was auditing one commentary on a Special Edition DVD of *Casablanca* and heard Roger Ebert aver that the characters in that film do not act "in selfish self-interest." Yea, verily.)

For this book, cultural archeologists Jeff Alexander and Tom Bissell have uncovered a cache of audio commentaries that shed a rare light on not just the pictures up for discussion but the commentators themselves; not to mention this ever-changing world in which we're livin'. How best should these commentaries be experienced? I imagine that one would start with two copies of the book (come on, they're cheap enough), two readers, the DVD, and you. Assign the part of one commentator to one reader, and the other to the other. (How you procure your readers is, of course, entirely your own business.) Pop in that DVD—make sure the volume on your home theater system is low. In about twenty minutes, whatever cute thing the animated menu does will be over, and you can press "Play Movie" and cue your readers. Now you're cooking. A great learning experience awaits. And remember: HAVE FUN.

To paraphrase Jorge Luis Borges in his story "Louis Menand, Author of the Quixote," Alexander and Bissell have, through their discoveries, enriched the halting and rudimentary art of listening.

—Glenn Kenny
Film Critic
Premiere Magazine

THE LORD OF THE RINGS:
THE FELLOWSHIP OF THE RING

[PLATINUM SERIES SPECIAL EXTENDED EDITION DVD]

Commentary by Howard Zinn and Noam Chomsky

Recorded August 2002

NOAM CHOMSKY: The film opens with Galadriel speaking. "The world has changed," she tells us, "I can feel it in the water." She's actually stealing a line from the nonhuman Treebeard, who says this to *her* near the end of *The Return of the King*, the novel. Already we can see whom is favored by this narrative and whom is not.

HOWARD ZINN: Right. "The world has changed." Of course, the main thing one learns when watching this film is that the world hasn't changed. Not at all.

Chomsky: We should examine carefully what's being established here in the prologue. For one, the point is clearly made that the "master ring," the so-called "one ring to rule them all," is actually a rather elaborate justification for preemptive war on Mordor.

Zinn: I think that's correct. Tolkien makes no attempt to hide the fact that rings are wielded by many of the ethnic enclaves in Middle Earth. The Dwarves have seven rings, the Elves have

3

three. The race of man has *nine* rings, for God's sake. There are at least nineteen rings floating around out there in Middle Earth, and yet Sauron's ring is supposedly so terrible that no one can be allowed to wield it. Why?

Chomsky: Notice too that the "war" being waged here is, evidently, in the land of Mordor itself—at the very base of Mount Doom. These terrible armies of Sauron, these dreadful demonized Orcs, have not proved very successful at conquering the neighboring realms—if that is even what Sauron was seeking to do. It seems fairly far-fetched.

Zinn: And observe the map device here—how the map is itself completely Gondor-centric. Rohan and Gondor are treated as though they are the literal center of Middle Earth. Obviously this is because men are living there. What of places such as Anfalas and Forlindon, or Near Harad? And this so-called map casually reveals other places—the Lost Realm, the Northern Waste—lost to whom? wasted how?—but tells us nothing about them. It's as though the people who live in these places are despicable and unworthy of mention. Who is producing this tale? What is their agenda? What are their interests and how are those interests being served by this portrayal? Questions we need to ask repeatedly.

Chomsky: And here comes Bilbo Baggins. Now this is, to my mind, where the story begins to reveal its deeper truths. In the books we learn that Saruman has been spying on Gandalf for years. And he wonders why Gandalf travels so incessantly to the Shire. As Tolkien himself wrote, the Shire's surfeit of pipeweed is one of the major reasons for Gandalf's continued visits.

Zinn: You view the conflict as being primarily about pipeweed, do you not?

Chomsky: Well, what we see here, in Hobbiton, is farmers tilling crops. The thing we have to remember is that the crop they are tilling is, in fact, pipeweed, an addictive drug transported and sold throughout Middle Earth for great profit.

Zinn: This is absolutely established in the books. Pipeweed is something all the Hobbits abuse. Gandalf is smoking it constantly. You are correct when you point out that Middle Earth depends on pipeweed in some crucial sense, but I think you may be overstating its importance. Clearly the war is not based only on the Shire's pipeweed. Rohan and Gondor's unceasing hunger for violence is a larger culprit, I would say.

Chomsky: But without the pipeweed, Middle Earth would fall apart. Saruman is trying to break up Gandalf's pipeweed ring. He's trying to divert it.

Zinn: Well, you know, it would be manifestly difficult to believe in magic rings unless everyone was high on pipeweed. So, clearly, it is in Gandalf's best interest to keep the inhabitants of Middle Earth hooked.

Chomsky: How do you think these wizards build gigantic towers and mighty fortresses? Where do they get the money? Keep in mind that I do not especially regard anyone, Saruman included, as an agent for progressivism. But obviously the pipeweed operation that exists is the dominant influence in Middle Earth. It's not some ludicrous magical ring.

Zinn: You've mentioned in the past the various flavors of pipeweed that Hobbits have cultivated: Gold Leaf, Old Toby, etc.

Chomsky: Nothing better illustrates the sophistication of the pipeweed economy than the fact that there are different brand names associated with the pipeweed. Ah, here we have Gandalf smoking a pipe in his wagon—the first of many clues that link us to the hidden undercurrents of power.

Zinn: Gandalf is deeply implicated. That's true. And of course the ring lore begins with him. He's the one who leaks this news of the supposed evil ring.

Chomsky: Now here, just before Bilbo's eleventy-first birthday party, we can see some symptoms of addiction. We are supposed to attribute Bilbo's tiredness, his sensation of feeling like "too little butter spread out on a piece of bread," to this magical ring he supposedly has. It's clear something else may be at work here.

Zinn: And soon Gandalf is delighting the Hobbits with his magic. Sauron's magic is somehow terrible, but Gandalf's, you'll notice, is wonderful.

Chomsky: And note how Gandalf's magic is based on gunpowder, on explosions.

Zinn: One can always delight the little people with explosions.

Chomsky: And it is interesting, too, that Gandalf's so-called magic is technological, and yet technology seems to be what condemns Saruman's enterprises as well as those of the Orcs.

Zinn: Exactly.

Chomsky: But we will address that later. Here we have Pippin and Merry stealing a bunch of fireworks and setting them off. This might be closer to the true heart of the Hobbits.

Zinn: You mean the Hobbits' natural inclination?

Chomsky: The Hobbits are criminals, essentially. Now we come to Bilbo's disappearance. Again, we have to question the validity of the ring and the magic powers attributed to it. Did Bilbo Baggins really disappear at his party, or is this some kind of mass hallucination attributable to a group of intoxicated Hobbits?

When forced to consider so-called magic compared with the hallucinatory properties of a known narcotic, Occam's Razor would indicate the latter as a far more plausible explanation.

Zinn: I also think it is a spectacular display of bad manners to disappear at your own birthday party. And here, for the first time, Gandalf speaks to Bilbo about magic rings. Still, it is never clearly established why this one ring is so powerful. Everything used to justify that belief is legendary.

Chomsky: Gandalf is clearly wondering if it's time to invoke his plan for the supposed revelation concerning the secret magic ring. Why now? Well, I suspect the people of Mordor—the Orcs, I'm speaking of—are starting to obtain some power, are starting to ask a little bit more from Middle Earth than Middle Earth has historically seen fit to give to them. And I don't think it's unreasonable for them to expect something back from Middle Earth after all they've been through. Of course, if that happened, the entire economy would be disrupted.

Zinn: The pipeweed-based economy.

Chomsky: And, as you noted, the military-industrial complex that exists in Gondor and Rohan. This constant state of alertness. This constant state of fear. And here Gandalf reveals *his* true nature.

Zinn: Indeed. Gandalf darkens the room and yells at poor Bilbo for understandably accusing him of trying to steal his ring.

Chomsky: Gandalf knows the ring is powerless. It's interesting that he attaches so much importance to it and yet will not pick it up himself. This is because he knows that merely possessing the worthless ring will not help his cause. It's important to keep others thinking that it can. If Gandalf held the ring, he might be asked to do something with it. But its magic is nonexistent.

Zinn: Well, power needs to have its proxies. That way the damage is always deniable. As long as the Hobbits have the ring, no one will ever question the plot Gandalf has hatched. So here is the big scary ring, and all that happens when Gandalf moves to touch it is that he sees a big flaming eye. And notice it is a... different kind of eye—not like our eye.

Chomsky: Almost a catlike eye.

Zinn: It's on fire. Somehow being an on-fire eye is this terrible thing in the minds of those in Middle Earth. I think this is a way of telling others in Middle Earth to be ashamed of their eyes. And of course you see the Orcs' eyes also look strange. They're this terrible color. And what does Gandalf tell Frodo about the ring? "Keep it secret. Keep it safe."

Chomsky: Yes. "Let's leave the most powerful object in all of Middle Earth with a weak little Hobbit, a race known for its chattering and intoxication, and tell him to keep it a secret." It's absurd.

Zinn: Right. And here is our first glimpse of the supposedly dreadful Mordor, which looks like a fairly functioning place.

Chomsky: This type of city is likely the best the Orcs can do if all they have are cliffs to build on. It's very impressive, in that sense.

Zinn: Especially considering the economic sanctions no doubt faced by Mordor. They must be dreadful. We see now that the Black Riders have been released, and they're going after Frodo. The *Black* Riders. Of course they're black. Everything evil is always black. And later Gandalf the Grey becomes Gandalf the White. Have you noticed that?

Chomsky: The most simplistic color symbolism, typical of such crude propaganda.

Zinn: And the writing on the ring, we learn here, is Orcish—the so-called "black speech." Orcish is evidently some spoliation of the language spoken in Rohan. This is what Tolkien says.

Chomsky: He explains that Orcish is a patois that developed during the Orcs' enslavement by Rohan, before they rebelled and left.

Zinn: Well, supposedly the Orcs were first bred by "the dark power of the north in the elder days." Tolkien says that "Orc" comes from the Mannish word *tark*, which means "man of Gondor."

Chomsky: Shameless, really.

Zinn: Gandalf mentions the evil stirring in Mordor. That's all he has to say. "It's evil." He doesn't elaborate on what's going on in Mordor, what the people are going through. They're evil because they're there.

Chomsky: I think the fact that we never actually see the enemy is quite damning. Then again, Gandalf is the greatest storyteller of all. He weaves tales that strand Middle Earth in a state of perpetual conflict. There's something of Kissinger in him, or vice-versa.

Zinn: He is celebrated on one hand as a great statesman and viewed by the people who understand the role that he *actually* plays as a dangerous lunatic and a war criminal. And notice that Gandalf's war pitch hits its highest note when the Black Riders arrive in Hobbiton. I don't think that's a coincidence.

Chomsky: This is Middle Earth's *Triumph of the Will*.

Zinn: And now Frodo and Sam are joined by Merry and Pippin, as they finally escape the Shire. They're being chased by the Black Riders. Again, if these Black Riders are so fearsome, and they can smell the ring so vividly, why don't they ever seem able to find the Hobbits when they're standing right next to them?

Chomsky: Well, they're on horseback.

Zinn: Right. And after an exciting dash, the Hobbits finally come to Bree. It seems they're very intolerant of outsiders at Bree. A clue there. They all gather at the Prancing Pony. If what we're told about Bree is true, it's no wonder that the pony is prancing.

Chomsky: Of course, like any city whose main trade is drugs, it's full of all sorts of undesirables. And here we are at the inn, thus beginning the second episode where the ring and its magical powers come to the fore.

Zinn: I think the Hobbits in this scene establish themselves as fairly heavy drinkers, fairly erratic people.

Chomsky: Yes, once more we have a roomful of inebriated people witnessing a miraculous event.

Zinn: Note how the ring's amazing, magical powers always manifest themselves in front of people who are completely intoxicated, part of the conspiracy, or else die violent deaths shortly thereafter.

Chomsky: This episode in Bree should cause us to ask, too, how much Frodo knows about the conspiracy. He seems to be piecing it together a little bit. I think at first he's an unwitting participant, fooled by Gandalf's propaganda.

Zinn: I'm much more suspicious of Frodo than you are. I've always viewed him as one of the most malevolent actors in this drama, precisely because of how he abets people like Gandalf.

Chomsky: And now, with Frodo in the midst of a hallucinogenic, paranoid state, we meet Strider.

Zinn: Note that the first thing he starts talking about is the ring. "That is no trinket you carry." A very telling irony, that. It is the kind of irony that Shakespeare would use. It is something Iago might say. And did you hear that? "Sauron the Deceiver." That is what Strider, the ranger with multiple names, calls Sauron. A ranger. I believe today we call them serial killers.

Chomsky: Or drug smugglers.

Zinn: And notice how Strider characterizes the Black Riders: "Neither living nor dead." Why, that's a useful enemy to have!

Chomsky: Yes. In this way you can never verify their existence, and yet they're horribly terrifying. We should not overlook the fact that Middle Earth is in a cold war at this moment, locked in perpetual conflict. Strider's rhetoric serves to keep fear alive.

Zinn: You've spoken to me before about Mordor's lack of access to the mineral wealth that the Dwarves control.

Chomsky: If we're going to get into the socio-economic reasons why certain structures develop in certain cultures... it's mainly geographical. We have Orcs in Mordor—trapped, with no mineral resources—hemmed in by the Ash Mountains, where the "free peoples" of Middle Earth can put a city, like Osgiliath, and effectively keep the border closed.

Zinn: Don't forget the Black Gate. The Black Gate, which, as Tolkien points out, was built by Gondor. And now we jump to the Orcs chopping down the trees in Isengard.

Chomsky: A terrible thing the Orcs do here, isn't it? They destroy nature. But again, what have we seen, time and time again?

Zinn: The Orcs have no resources. They're desperate.

Chomsky: Desperate people driven to do desperate things.

Zinn: Desperate to compete with the economic powerhouses of Rohan and Gondor.

Chomsky: This is a means to an end. And while that might not be the most prudent philosophy, it makes the race of Man in no way superior. Men and Elves are going to great lengths to hold on to their power. Two cultures locked in conflict over power, with one culture clearly suffering a great deal. I think sharing power and resources would have been the wisest approach, but Rohan and Gondor have shown no interest in doing so. Sometimes, revolution must be—

Zinn: Mistakes are often—

Chomsky: Blood must be shed. I forget what Thomas Jefferson—

Zinn: He said that blood was the—

Chomsky: The blood of tyrants—

Zinn: The blood of tyrants—

Chomsky: —waters the tree of—

Zinn: —revolution.

Chomsky: —freedom. Or revolution. Something like that.

Zinn: I think that's actually very, very close.

Chomsky: One of the problems with the perspective offered by the Man-Elf coalition is that you have to try so hard to get at the truth of the conflict, at what is really going on; it's so obscured by their propaganda and relentless militarism. I mean, here at Weathertop we have swords being distributed to the Hobbits by Strider so they can protect themselves against these "evil creatures." Now, in this case, it's probably warranted, though the "evil creatures" are looking for the ring in their own individual self-interest. They're behaving in a purely rational way.

Zinn: The Nazgûl have been ordered to get the ring, which they believe has magic powers. So that's what they're doing.

Chomsky: Sometimes valid rationality is forced into conflict because of the structures of culture. But working through those cultural differences is where the peace lies. It doesn't lie in destroying some magical ring. This takes me back to the media's involvement in all this—and the way they are being controlled by Gandalf, such as when he covers Saruman's palantir in Orthanc. This is the stone that allows one to interact with different cultures.

Zinn: Right. "What does the eye command, my lord?" This is what the Orcs ask Saruman. In other words, what does the palantir say? Clearly the Orcs know a lot more about the people of Rohan and Gondor than the people of Rohan and Gondor have ever cared to know about them. They're curious beings.

Chomsky: Naturally, it's in Rohan/Gondor's interest to keep the Orcs obscured and vilified. It's always the first step toward genocide. And is this—is there anything less than genocide being advocated in this film?

Zinn: I don't think so.

Chomsky: Is there any kind of idea that men should live in peace with the Orcs?

Zinn: Think of the scenes in the prologue with all the arrows hitting these thousands of Orcs. We're supposed to think that this is a good thing.

Chomsky: I think this is a tragedy, this story. Because it's about two cultures locked in conflict, victims all of poor leadership. It's a human tragedy *and* an Orcish tragedy.

Zinn: A perfect example of what you're talking about is here, when Strider attacks the Black Riders, "saving" Frodo from them.

Chomsky: Think of it from the Black Riders' perspective. No doubt they arrived at Weathertop thinking, "Can we ask a few questions? We'd like to talk to you."

Zinn: Now from here we jump to Isengard, post-ecological atrocities. The environmental degradation is regrettable, but I see some good things. I see industrialization, I see a very cooperative workforce, I see an empowered people who aren't terrorized, a people attempting to make do with what they have.

Chomsky: They're making weapons, which is sad. I mean, it would be nice if they could make plowshares, but unfortunately this isn't the time for plowshares. Still, the Orcs are showing great ingenuity, and, most importantly, they're showing cooperation. You're right about that.

Zinn: Actually it shows the Orcs smithing a lot of pieces of metal. I don't think it's necessarily established that they're making swords, is it? Those could be farming implements of some sort. They're definitely some type of peasant society. But I have to ask you, what about the genetic engineering that goes on with the Uruk-hai?

Chomsky: It's certainly a strange aspect of their culture, but why should we be so condemning? I mean, this is the way they reproduce. If it looks disgusting to us, well maybe we should readjust what we regard as disgusting. I mean, is that any more vile than pulling a baby out of a gaping, bloody hole?

Zinn: And we go back to the Hobbits. After Frodo's been stabbed, Strider and Sam immediately journey out in search of another herb: kingsfoil, or *athelas*.

Chomsky: Aragorn is evidently into Research and Development as well.

Zinn: He does seem knowledgeable of "herbs" and "medicines."

Chomsky: And notice how Arwen Evenstar greets Strider: a knife to the throat. That's a very telling, very interesting thing that happens over and over. Whenever "friendly" people encounter one another, they're raising swords, looking fearful and distrustful.

Zinn: Now we witness the Black Riders finally together—all nine Riders—giving chase to Arwen and Frodo. When we see the Orcs destroy their environment, it is this big scandal. But Arwen is able to send a whole herd of watery horses down a river, no doubt a very delicate ecosystem, and probably completely demolish it, and no one says anything about that.

Chomsky: The Elves, of course, always claim they're the best custodians of nature. And there's a curious type of nature-worship in their culture that allows them to claim, by every implication, that trees are more important than people. They don't even regard the Orcs as people. However, Orcs are thinking, sentient, conscious beings with a culture and a language. They feel pain. They express emotion. They are constantly evolving, trying to better themselves.

Zinn: But here the Elvish culture is revealed to be very elaborate, because, of course, they have better architecture. But I vastly prefer the real grittiness one finds in Mordor. Think of the suspiciously clean city of Rivendell. You don't see any life going on there. No people at all. It should be said, though, that on occasion the Orcs have been known to eat one another.

Chomsky: That's cannibalism, sure, but maybe it's part of a sacred ritual for them. Maybe it's an ancient part of their culture. Who are we to judge? Still, I have problems with it. I agree.

Zinn: So here we have another shot of Rivendell being beautiful because it happens to be located in the mountains, where the lighter people live. And we see here the two primary players moving the action forward: an Elf and a wizard. Elrond and Gandalf.

Chomsky: This is our first glimpse into the power structure of Middle Earth. It's basically two men who rule their people, deciding what will happen on their own, without consulting anybody else. Gandalf, even more disturbingly, does not even rule a people but rather rules from his own personal whims and preferences.

Zinn: Isn't it implied that he's from Rohan?

Chomsky: Originally he's from "over the sea." He is some type of magic spirit, according to his own myth about himself. He doesn't claim any land, instead acting as custodian of all of their lands. Of course, I think he's a classic dictator, pulling the strings. Can you detect how outraged I am by this?

Zinn: Why do you suppose it is that the Elves don't want the ring to stay in Rivendell? Isn't this obvious proof that the ring is nothing but a device to be used against Mordor?

Chomsky: This is their justification for war. That's why Boromir is so insightful when he says, basically, "Why don't we use it? If this ring's so great, who don't we use the damn thing?"

Zinn: And what happens to Boromir? The Orcs are tricked into killing him. Thus silencing him.

Chomsky: I think this is an interesting scene—Aragorn in Rivendell looking upon the Isildur mural—because it shows how the militarization of their propaganda has fed their cultural behaviors and religious beliefs.

Zinn: Isildur's broken sword, you mean?

Chomsky: The myth. I mean, look at this museum, this cult, all based around a broken sword. They've developed a religion so that people can be effectively marshaled into battle. And Aragorn is a part of that. He's a king, performing a ceremony for people to continue this senseless belief in some kind of genetic superiority. It is rather like saying, "I have the signet ring of the house of the czar," or something. "Now I can rule."

Zinn: Well, I think this scene shows us what kind of person Aragorn is—a loner, possibly a drug lord.

Chomsky: And then we get bathed in Aragorn-Arwen love lore. And it's the·most simplistic kind of propaganda. You've got this beautiful woman who represents the Party, represents the people of the Motherland, and you have the hero. Develop a little love affair between them.

Zinn: A love affair between the putative hero and the personified Motherland concept, you mean.

Chomsky: Right. The humans are all so entranced by the Elves' completely mythological power. It's a spell that has been cast upon them.

Zinn: I see the humans, embodied by Aragorn, as being indicative of a sort of middle-class longing.

Chomsky: It keeps them striving. If you're a good enough man, you can be an Elf.

Zinn: An Elf. As if that's the best thing to be.

Chomsky: Now, at the Council of Elrond, we have the Middle Earth equivalent of a television broadcast. It's one guy sitting in a tall chair and talking at twenty other people. This is how information is spread in this culture. But, you know, it doesn't have to be this way. Imagine that, right now, you have the people in Gondor with a palantir, the people in Rohan with a palantir, the people in the Woodland Realm with a palantir. And everyone could be standing around it, talking to one another, sharing a conference in which the people have an equal interest and stake in what decisions are made.

Zinn: Technology that Gandalf already knows is available. But do we see a single Orc?

Chomsky: Oh, of course not. Of course not. Because everyone here has a vested interest in keeping the Orcs down.

Zinn: Boromir is the only one honest enough to talk about what the real story is here.

Chomsky: Boromir's an interesting case. His realm is threatened by the Orcs in a very immediate way. But he's also seen that this occupation of Orc land is engendered by his people's own aggressive policies. So he's like an enlightened Israeli who looks at his enemies and thinks, "If I were in their situation, I would be just like them." Because, in a sense, he is.

Zinn: My God. Look at this. Keep in mind that these are supposed to be Middle Earth's enlightened people at this council, and they're all fighting; they all hate one another.

Chomsky: It's just so complicated, the webs of relationships.

Zinn: Now Frodo, son of Drogo, agrees to take the ring to Mount Doom. Something tells me that no one in Mordor calls it Mount Doom.

Chomsky: And everyone baits Frodo into this. "You are our agent, going on a suicide mission. You have to do it for the Motherland."

Zinn: So is Frodo the Mohamed Atta figure in this story?

Chomsky: He's a fanatical true believer. And crazy. Obviously, totally insane.

Zinn: And hear what Aragorn tells Frodo: "You have my sword."

Chomsky: So militaristic.

Zinn: Notice that no one says, "You have my diplomatic skills." I think the only real diplomat of Middle Earth is Gollum. He's the only one who makes any meaningful, cross-cultural exchange with any of these people—being a torture victim at the hand of the Orcs and his attempted strangulation of the Hobbits.

Chomsky: I think of Gollum as more of a deluded madman, one more sinned against than sinned.

Zinn: There's room for argument. And, yet again, here we see Bilbo ravaged from the effects of pipeweed. It's been flushed from his system in his idyll-cum-rehab in Rivendell. And what does he give Frodo? He gives him his sword, of course. *Sting*, and his mithril vest.

Chomsky: As if to say, "You know, when you've stabbed enough people in the back like I have, you'll need this shirt of mithril." Hobbits are bandits. They have this veneer of nobility around them, but they are nothing more than demented little thieves.

Zinn: Now, we see in Moria that the Dwarves had a fairly sophisticated mithril mine. Wouldn't you say the Dwarves are the Jew-like figures of Middle Earth?

Chomsky: They are former slaves. The comparison is apt.

Zinn: They're good at doing things with their hands. This is something Tolkien is very adamant about. They're useful, but they're not very educated. Ah, and this is also where we first see Gollum. I stick to my view of Gollum as a rebel who transgresses boundaries. In many ways he is the heroic, empathetic conscience of this story. He's the only one who cares about bridging the gaps between these many cultures.

Chomsky: You could be right. There's possibly something very wise about Gollum. Obviously he's well traveled; he's a pilgrim.

Zinn: I think his sexuality is questionable, and that's why he's viewed as this hateful, awful thing. Everyone always talks about killing him.

Chomsky: Gandalf of course likes to have as many ghosts around him as possible. He slyly encourages Frodo in this belief that Gollum is some kind of horrible, corrupt thing. He neglects to say, "You know, I tortured him just a couple of months ago."

Zinn: Exactly.

Chomsky: At Balin's tomb notice that Gandalf doesn't give anybody else the supposed Dwarf chronicle to read. Gandalf could be passing it off as Balin's last words. We don't know what is actually recorded in it, though. Very cunning. It could be agreement drawn up between the Orcs and the Dwarves. It could quite easily be that.

Zinn: It would explain why he kept it out of Gimli's hands.

Chomsky: Sure—"No, don't worry. *I'll* read it. Let me read this to you guys."

Zinn: What I think this reveals is that the Dwarves have a very beautiful, elegant, poetic way about them.

Chomsky: Except Gandalf could be making it all up.

Zinn: That's what I mean. This is much more of a Gandalfian, flowery prose. It's hard to imagine the Dwarves writing that way.

Chomsky: And now the terrible Orcs invade Balin's tomb. Let's be clear about a few things here. The Orcs have established a home in Moira. They are fighting a war of self-defense against the invading Fellowship. It's fairly clear that the Orcs are hiding, because if they go outside, they have every reason to believe that they will be massacred by Gandalf.

Zinn: The Orcs certainly don't seem to be very good fighters, do they? If they're such a terrible, evil, warlike culture—

Chomsky: They can't kill even one of these little Hobbits who just received their swords only a few days ago. One would think that if the Orcs were as bad as the corrupt Man-Elf coalition says, they would be a lot better at fighting. It lends credence to the peasant hypothesis—that they were trying to scrabble out a meager existence in the land of Mordor.

Zinn: You can see here, too, that the way the Hobbits fight is highly indicative of their culture: They jump on a wounded foe and then stab him in the neck.

Chomsky: They're very morally ambiguous characters. There's a nasty complacency about Hobbits. One would think that they could, easily enough, find out about all of the things that happen in the world—all of the consequences of their pipeweed-growing actions. And now Middle Earth's power structure is revealing itself, and they're a part of it. Still, they don't question it. Worse yet, they revel in it.

Zinn: My question is: How hard would the mithril have to be to stop the cave troll from piercing you with his spear?

Chomsky: Possibly mithril once served the same function in Middle Earth culture as pipeweed does now. After all, you have to keep creating new industries.

Zinn: Of course. The culture of consumption is founded upon whatever the new thing happens to be. One day it's mithril; the next day it's pipeweed. Perhaps tomorrow it will be kingsfoil?

Chomsky: Here again we have the Orcs running after the Fellowship. The Orcs, apparently, are going to slaughter them, and in my estimation they would be well within their rights to do so. But do they? No, they do not. They stop.

Zinn: They stop.

Chomsky: And then they run away because the Balrog comes out. Take note of the fact that the Orcs don't appear to like the Balrog much themselves. They're scared of it.

Zinn: I'm not sure what role the Balrog really plays in this.

Chomsky: I think it just happened to be there, guarding its own little part of the mine.

Zinn: And look at these Orcs! Supposedly so evil and vicious, and yet they don't do anything. They even appear to talk it over amongst themselves.

Chomsky: Look at it from their perspective: They've been locked up in this cave. They're frightened. They know they're not good fighters. They're just a undeveloped peasant society.

Zinn: As evidenced by their crude, ungainly weapons.

Chomsky: Perhaps they've been radicalized a bit. But I doubt they are true evildoers.

Zinn: Again, I'm not sure what role the Balrog plays.

Chomsky: I, too, am uncertain on that point. They're considered to be one big gang, but I don't think a credible link has been established between the Orcs and the Balrog.

Zinn: Agreed. Based on available evidence, the Balrog and Orcs are mortal enemies. Here, very significantly, is the Bridge of Khazad-Dûm. You will notice that what is destroyed is a bridge—another potential connector.

Chomsky: On a symbolic level, that is a very good point.

Zinn: All the borders in this film are constantly being destroyed, or overrun, or eliminated, or sealed. It's all about fear—fearing the other. Notice, too, that the Elf Legolas jumps across the ruined bridge first.

Chomsky: They'll cross this bridge, and the bridge will collapse, and they'll never be able to communicate with the Balrog again or with the Orcs inside. In fact, they're sealing off the Orcs from ever escaping. They're leaving the Orcs in the cave with this big Balrog. Now again, surely among these Moria Orcs were some Orc radicals—aggressive, angry, militant radicals. We shouldn't understate that.

Zinn: Well, look how the Orcs grow up. What do you expect?

Chomsky: I mean, what other options have they?

Zinn: I dare say that, were I an Orc, I might possibly be one of those terrorist Orcs, shooting arrows at the Fellowship myself.

Chomsky: Here comes the Balrog. Notice Gandalf's unilateral action. "Quick, get away! I have to fight this thing alone!"

Zinn: Once again, you see a creature that's on fire being demonized in this movie: the flaming eye, the flaming Balrog. As though being on fire is this terrible affliction to have.

Chomsky: As though they can help it if they're on fire.

Zinn: After Gandalf falls, you get another view of the so-called terrorist Orcs. You know, the regrettable side of the Orcs does occasionally come out. The violence. It doesn't help their cause when these distinct, individual Orcs take it upon themselves to lash out at the inequality of the system. But even these violent Orcs don't seem happy. They're not pleased with themselves. It's a violence borne of necessity.

Chomsky: Sure. They're trapped in a cycle of violence.

Zinn: And now we come to Galadriel's wood, Lothlorien. The film—inexcusably, in my view—leaves out a lot of the things that happen to Gimli in this sequence.

Chomsky: He's forced to wear a blindfold. He is not allowed to see the Elves. This is the apartheid system the Fellowship serves.

Zinn: And even here the Elves hold arrows to his head. He's completely brutalized. But of course Gimli falls in love with Galadriel, thus perpetuating the Dwarves' self-hatred.

Chomsky: It's similar to the method the Elves use to ensnare men like Aragorn. The Elves want to be worshiped. A kind of brainwashing occurs whenever anyone is exposed to their culture.

Zinn: I mean, look at how the Elves greet people: with arrows. Is that so different from the Orcs?

Chomsky: Right. And they're supposed to be nature-worshippers. It's sort of sickening and very bourgeois.

Zinn: And of course Galadriel is wearing a ring throughout this entire scene. She has a ring—arguably the most powerful ring. Somehow she's trusted to wield this power responsibly. This woman who reads people's minds without asking them.

Chomsky: That's true. She constantly invades other people's thoughts. Of course you have to give the Elves credit for women's rights. But we learn here that even if you cede women these rights, they become just as morally culpable as any man. And have you taken proper note of Galadriel's farewell gesture? It is some sort of *Sieg Heil* gesture.

Zinn: It is vaguely reminiscent of the biomechanics of National Socialism. You'll notice, too, how clearly the Man-Elf coalition controls all the modes of transportation in Middle Earth. We always see the Orcs running. But Legolas, Gimli, and Aragorn— I mean, sometimes they are riding horses. The Orcs have nothing like any of this. The Orcs certainly don't canoe.

Chomsky: Well, they don't have these wide, beautiful rivers to canoe on. Instead, just as you say, the Orcs are always seen running. A bunch of farmers, holding their clumsy weapons.

Zinn: The white hand of Saruman on the heads of the Uruk-hai. Of course, the hand in control is white. And, good lord—these giant statues on the Anduin River. The Sentinels of Númenor. These huge, monolithic statues with their hands thrust forever up. I can intuit what these sentinels are saying: "Stay away, Orcs."

Chomsky: "Keep out of our land."

Zinn: "Keep out of our land. Don't come in." It is little wonder that the Orcs are so warlike and angry.

Chomsky: And of course the sentinels are holding swords. More monolithic images of supposedly noble militarism.

Zinn: One suspects that Orc slaves probably built the things. I imagine there's a lot of Orc labor that gets in through Gondor and Rohan. They want to get out of Mordor. There are simply not a lot of economic options for them there.

Chomsky: This simple bunch of peasants, hastily rallied together against these well-armed, well-equipped Elves and men.

Zinn: And now the Orcs face Aragorn for the first time. It's not very obvious what's happening. The Orcs appear rather skittish.

Chomsky: Well, some of these Orcs are charging. It is fairly easy to imagine what they are feeling. They've seen this ranger's work before. Aragorn has so many names, it is all but certain that he has a few Orcish names as well. "Orc-Killer," perhaps. "Orc-Slayer." "Madman"? Look at all this casual slaughter.

Zinn: We know the Orcs have a hand in murdering Boromir, but Aragorn's innocence isn't clearly established. I think he maneuvered Boromir into that position to get him out of the way. After all, Boromir had a definite claim on Aragorn's supposed kingship.

Chomsky: That is very possible.

Zinn: I have to ask, what does this story do for the powerful? For one, it makes them feel very good about the kind of things they've done to less powerful societies. The way they exploit them and the way they invent these phony pretexts to wage wars of aggression against them. The powerful need to tell themselves these stories.

Chomsky: And yet, as in all stories of this type, hidden within the story are the keys to unlocking the hidden modes of power.

Zinn: The thing is, though, that even when the dominant culture itself tells the story, the story cannot help but include those tell-tale signifiers of power that surrender the true nature of the story.

Chomsky: No matter how often the storyteller obscures the truth, the truth will come out because it's embedded in their language.

Zinn: Thankfully, the literature of oppression can never last because the oppression is always so obvious. And the people who are suppressed grow increasingly aware of how they're suppressed. And once they're aware of how suppressed they are, they can—

Chomsky: Right, they're able to—

Zinn: We've got to get our conspiracy straight.

Chomsky: Not necessarily. Think of Lee Harvey Oswald.

Zinn: A patsy. A CIA agent.

Chomsky: A cold-blooded, ruthless killer.

Zinn: Right.

Chomsky: He was a good shot. He was a bad shot.

Zinn: Right. Exactly.

Chomsky: But then, I don't really believe in conspiracy theories about JFK.

Zinn: Neither do I.

Chomsky: So...

Zinn: Isn't that funny?

ALIENS

[SPECIAL RED-STATE EDITION DVD]

Commentary by Dinesh D'Souza and Ann Coulter

Recorded May 2003

DINESH D'SOUZA: I want to thank the people at FOX and News Corp for inviting us to contribute a commentary to this excellent film. Far too often DVD commentaries exhibit a distinctly liberal bias.

ANN COULTER: I agree. I think it's basically endemic of the hegemonic leftist control of all forms of media expression—burying conservative subtexts beneath a lot of lefty cuddling. Now, as the titles come up, perhaps we should discuss the first *Alien* movie. I see that film as evidencing the insidious effects of a creeping, dangerous worldview slowly infecting a small group of people and then, one by one, destroying them. Not unlike, say, liberalism.

D'SOUZA: I see your point there, and I don't disagree. I think there's an interesting thing going on in *Alien*. I like to think of these movies as reflecting the presidents who were in office when they came out. As I'm sure you remember, *Alien* dramatizes an impotent response to an unknown threat—that threat being, of course, the alien. A single alien, with the help of a quisling android, murders an entire crew.

Coulter: With the exception of Ripley, let's remember. She's independent, strong, and tall.

D'Souza: Extremely tall.

Coulter: A very Phyllis Schlafly-like figure.

D'Souza: To get back to my earlier point, we shouldn't forget that Carter was president at that time. One word: malaise. We all know what Carter did to this country.

Coulter: Screwed it seven ways to Sunday. The liberal contribution to America is essentially worthless. During the Carter years it was actually worse than worthless.

D'Souza: Now, we open with Ripley asleep in some sort of cryostasis after having escaped the *Nostromo*'s last terrible voyage in *Alien*.

Coulter: Ripley here, alone and drifting through space, reminds me of Nemo aboard the *Nautilus* in *20,000 Leagues Under the Sea*. There are a lot of similarities between the two, in fact. That film was about destroying strange animals too. Here we follow along with a remote-controlled camera peaking into Ripley's escape pod, which has been adrift for many years. So, obviously, this is the future.

D'Souza: Look at the impressive technology. We can already see the great leap from the world of the preceding film to this one. This is the Reagan world. This is a world of incredible technology and administrative competence with deep faith in its military prowess. A utopia.

Coulter: How well do we suppose Ripley will adapt from a sad, paranoid Carter world to an efficient, powerful Reagan world?

D'Souza: I don't think I could put myself in the mind of a woman!

Coulter: Notice when Burke comes to the hospital to see Ripley, he's wearing a very snappy—and very appealing—outfit. Very hip. Very Chess King.

D'Souza: I like this guy, too. It's a welcome relief to have a character in the *Alien* movies clean-shaven and looking sharp. He's wearing a suit, he's washed his hair. He seems like someone you can trust.

Coulter: Notice, though, that Ripley's cat doesn't especially like Burke. The cat could be a liberal. It wouldn't surprise me. What Burke understands is something some stupid cat never will: People are essentially horrible. Enlightened people are and must be out for themselves. Sorry, liberals! But it's true.

D'Souza: Now we're having an apparent dream sequence. Ripley's giving birth to an alien here. This is some kind of nightmare flashback—we've all had them—to 1979.

Coulter: I think of this as the film's abortion subtext, something that, unbelievably, no one has thought to address. What I think this movie is doing is showing Ripley—who, in her nightmares, imagines she has been impregnated by an alien—slowly coming to terms with the fact that, during an abortion, someone dies. In this case, when the alien bursts out of her stomach, that someone is Ripley.

D'Souza: Or perhaps the alien represents Ripley's unconscious recognition of the life within her hostile womb? This shows her reeducation from the pathological hostility she has, previously, shown for the Corporation's capitalism and traditional morality.

Coulter: Yes. There's this typically liberal refusal to think of abortion as a real action involving the annihilation of a living thing. Ripley is coming into her own as a conservative hero. And it's breathtaking. I don't know if I can wait to see her start wasting aliens. What do you think of the future as it's so far been shown? Personally, I like it a lot.

D'Souza: Well, it certainly looks like business and technology have really done an excellent job providing for the needs and cares of the citizenry.

Coulter: Absolutely. I detect the hand of distinctly private enterprise in that medical frigate. If it were a government medical frigate, I can only imagine all the freeloading, obese people loitering around in the hallways.

D'Souza: And look at the splendid, bucolic backdrop Ripley's looking at here. How beautiful the Earth looks in the future. I think there's a lesson here for those alarmist, organic-farming, fruit-juice-drinking, garbage-sorting enviro-nuts who—

Coulter: That's actually a TV screen Ripley is looking at. Those trees aren't real.

D'Souza: Well, it's a great simulation, an ingenious solution.

Coulter: Again, here: Burke in a *very* natty red tie. And he really fills out a pair of chinos.

D'Souza: We're watching how he tries to help Ripley help herself, by convincing her to get back on the bike and revisit an alien-infested planet. Just in case anybody thought that conservatism and compassion couldn't go hand in hand—

Coulter: Burke?

D'Souza: Yeah, look at him. He's clearly got Ripley's best interests in mind.

Coulter: I think so.

D'Souza: Or, if not, then he's got the best interests of the Corporation in mind.

Coulter: Of course he does.

D'Souza: Would Ripley have gotten that great medical care without the Corporation?

Coulter: Absolutely not.

D'Souza: I don't think so.

Coulter: No.

D'Souza: Would she have a job without the Corporation?

Coulter: She wouldn't.

D'Souza: Would she have any purpose in this movie without the Corporation?

Coulter: Lieutenant Ripley?

D'Souza: Yes.

Coulter: No, not without Burke.

D'Souza: Not without Burke.

Coulter: You'll notice, too, that Ripley doesn't need any twenty-third-century Gloria Steinem to tell her that she has worth or is a meaningful person. She just does it on her own. She doesn't need any external cultural validation.

D'Souza: She could clean herself up a bit better. Don't you think?

Coulter: Perhaps.

D'Souza: Ripley's got a little bit of... you know, she looks like the head of a women's studies department.

Coulter: I violently disagree. Ripley's style is slightly mannish. But that's her right as a woman. Look at Barbara Bush. Mannish women are often better soldiers. Let's talk about this scene, though, this *fantastic* boardroom scene, in which the board members discuss with Ripley the Corporation's alien policy. Two things: We see that Ripley is 1) a take-charge woman but certainly not a whining feminist; and 2) completely unrepentant about the destruction of the alien in the first film. If certain cultures—for example, the alien's—are going to be hostile to your own, then they have to be either Christianized or destroyed.

D'Souza: You listen to liberals today and they talk about this kind of species equivalency. You know, "All species are equally good." Anybody who believes that should try going to live with those species. When I first came to the United States, I met this crazy, smelly guy on the Dartmouth campus who told me how wonderful it must have been to grow up in India. I said, "You think India's so great, why don't you try living there?"

Coulter: Still, I think Ripley is within her rights to be angry here.

D'Souza: Angry with the Corporation?

Coulter: Angry is maybe not the best word. *Frustrated*, rather, that the Corporation does not yet realize how important alien annihilation really is. Ripley's larger point is that the Corporation does not yet appreciate the danger. Naturally, the Corporation has everyone's best interest in mind—*given the information that it has now.*

D'Souza: It will devise a method of dealing with these problems. Initially it might not always be the best method—

Coulter: But it will get there. That's how capitalism works. Self-interest, rationality—

D'Souza: If this Corporation's board makes some ghastly mistake that brings back a rabid alien that's going to destroy the world, well, then a new board will be appointed that won't make the same mistake. And in this film we'll see the integration of two skill sets: the Corporation's resources, power, and technology used in concert with the righteous anger and imperialist might of Ripley's related project to eradicate another species.

Coulter: Uniquely conservative impulses—intelligent financial self-preservation, moral righteousness, and the understanding that threatening alien ideologies need to be ruthlessly crushed—do come together beautifully in the movie. And look at this. Here we have one of the additional scenes cut from the film's theatrical release. What are we seeing? We're seeing the brave, hard-working people in the colony that the aliens ultimately destroy.

D'Souza: They're a colony, right? They're terra-forming this life-less planet?

Coulter: Absolutely.

D'Souza: They're trying to make this planet habitable for humans.

Coulter: Perhaps trying to Christianize the aliens as well.

D'Souza: I think they thought the aliens were past Christianizing.

Coulter: "The Wayland Atomic Corp: Building Better Worlds." That's the admirable motto of this company. And here's little Newt, the young girl Ripley eventually rescues, who's shown in these regretfully deleted scenes to be a real go-getter. She's the recipient of the colony's Second Grade Citizenship Award, for instance. Imagine the great work this colony could have done had the aliens not destroyed them!

D'Souza: Well, there is a cautionary element to this tale, which is, "Always be better prepared than your enemy is for battle." If only liberals understood the importance of military preparation.

Coulter: Finally! The Marines! Coming out of their cryostasis. And Burke is with them, thank goodness. He knows what's at stake here.

D'Souza: Let's talk about Burke for a moment, because he's a complicated figure here. Does wanting to get rich by betraying your friends, or opportunistically using the Marines, necessarily make you a bad guy? Of course not. Indeed, I would go further. The rich are in the best position to be the good guys because only the rich have the resources necessary to be of help to those in need.

Coulter: Technological capitalism, not government, is the true catalyst for equality.

D'Souza: That's right.

Coulter: And technological capitalism is *exactly* what this movie is about. There's no government even mentioned in this movie. These Marines are corporate Marines—though Frost, encouragingly, does have an American flag stitched on his shoulder. So does the Marine's leader, Gorman. So we see that this future military is, also promisingly, subject to a rational, profit-driven Corporation—not some meddling, do-gooder government. Do you think that a liberal government would even *respond* to the alien-human genocide on this planet? No. They'd want some multistellar force to "investigate." Like aliens, liberals hate human beings. But imagine if the aliens were attacking each other and destroying precious alien culture. Then, naturally, the liberals would be hysterical. *Then* they would send in the Marines.

D'Souza: Sacrificing good human lives.

Coulter: And good bullets, too, frankly. We're going to squander some good M-80 rounds to preserve an alien culture? Conservatives take care of their own. Like Newt. This is a tough little girl. She knows what life is about.

D'Souza: In trying circumstances, she shows resilience and a can-do spirit. She doesn't wait for someone else to take care of her.

Coulter: People are victimized by aliens because they allow themselves to be victimized by aliens. But I have to ask: Which of the Marines is your favorite?

D'Souza: I think I'd have to go with Corporal Hicks. He's an all-American guy.

Coulter: As much as I admire the Marines, I have to say that this Captain Gorman is a disaster. A liberal disaster. He has no idea what he's doing. Right now he's mistakenly telling Ripley that an area recently infested with hostile liberal aliens is secure. But Ripley knows the truth. She knows how insidious these aliens are. Once you let them through your borders, they'll do everything that they can to destroy your society because they hate liberty.

D'Souza: I think that the Corporation is quite prudently investigating the source of these problems: aliens.

Coulter: They're not putting aliens in zoos. They're not trying to understand them.

D'Souza: They're not talking to them. They're putting them in petri dishes and cutting them up and putting them under microscopes. This is where Newt pops up and is almost shot. Again, I can only imagine what a liberal would do with Newt in this situation. Probably discard her as cavalierly as an unborn child. For a liberal, Newt's barely old enough to be a real person.

Coulter: But Ripley chases Newt into a garbage chute, finding, among other things, Newt's Second Grade Citizenship Award. What are we seeing here? I think we're seeing compassion—conservative compassion. Liberal compassion is primarily a matter of telling poor people they're not to blame for their poverty, telling women they're not to blame when they kill their unborn children. But Ripley is reaching into herself and finding the warmth that women naturally have for children.

D'Souza: Let's just hope she finds a father to help raise Newt by the end of this movie.

Coulter: Well, of course. Hicks, perhaps?

D'Souza: We certainly can't have her raising a child alone.

Coulter: Look at the expression on Ripley's face when she finds Newt's Citizenship Award. Pride. This is an enterprising, academically successful young woman.

D'Souza: Citizenship. It's a wonderful virtue to be extolling. And it looks like she's been ravaged. The liberal alien infestation has almost completely damaged her.

Coulter: Did you hear that? "Come on… we're wasting our time." That's what Gorman says when he's faced with this little girl, the last survivor. Poor Newt. Newt is heartbreaking, I have to say. Newts will always break your heart. Always.

D'Souza: And she plays with a doll—Casey. It's nice to know that playing with dolls isn't stigmatized in this future for a young lady. Newt has just learned a hard lesson about the reality of life.

Coulter: That aliens will kill your family?

D'Souza: Yes. As Hobbes says, "Life is solitary, poor, nasty, brutish, and short." And constantly terrorized by aliens.

Coulter: Frankly, I don't like Bishop, the android—or, as he puts it, in a nauseating example of twenty-third-century political correctness, the "artificial person"—who is seen here dissecting one of the hateful face-hugging alien egg-implanters. "Magnificent creatures." That's what he calls them. Whose side is he on?

D'Souza: I'd say it's an example of the widely known liberal tendency to aestheticize evil—if I believed that liberals had a concept of evil at all.

Coulter: Now the Marines discover that there are a lot of good, upright colonists still alive in the cooling towers. And they have to go rescue them.

D'Souza: They're the right people for the job. Who else would you send—the United Planets?

Coulter: What do you think of the shoulder-mounted security cameras that each of the soldiers has?

D'Souza: The only problem is that there aren't enough of them.

Coulter: We need to talk about something, though. What do we think could have been done differently in this cooling-tower rescue mission, which ends so tragically, as a kind of interstellar Mogadishu, with the loss of so many brave Corporation Marines?

D'Souza: Well, unlike a lot of armchair generals we saw during a recent war, I'm not going to pretend I have any kind of military expertise—particularly twenty-third-century military expertise—but I think that a long, sustained air campaign followed by modest use of ground force would have been enough.

Coulter: That's the nice thing about wiping everything out with air strikes. You don't have to spend a lot of money rebuilding.

D'Souza: If nothing is left alive, you don't have to build a school.

Coulter: Did I call what's coming up an "interstellar Mogadishu"?

D'Souza: Yes, you did. And apparently they brought the wrong bullets. It's pointed out, as the Marines embark on their cooling-tower rescue mission, that they can't shoot anything within the towers because the whole site is one big fusion reactor. This is one of the first mistakes that doom the mission to failure.

Coulter: It's not Hicks's fault. It's Gorman's. Hicks has a shotgun. And I have to say, my heart sort of pitter-patters when he cocks it. I just like the sound. Oh, my. Here the Corporation Marines have stumbled across a wall-implanted nest of dead and near-dead colonists. My question about this sequence is this: If a woman is pregnant with an alien, does she have the right to an abortion?

D'Souza: That's a tricky one.

Coulter: Because we see here that some of the colonists have, in fact, been impregnated by aliens.

D'Souza: I'm going to make an uncharacteristic admission for both of us: This is a tough, complicated issue. On the one hand, you have these unborn aliens, and their lives are sacred. But, really, these humans are in no way equipped to take care of them adequately once they're born.

Coulter: So they should go ahead and give birth to the alien, but destroy it immediately afterward?

D'Souza: I think so, yes.

Coulter: We see *here* that Corporal Dietrich finds a still-living colonist. She is, regretfully, pregnant with an alien. Correct me if I'm wrong, but this colonist sounds like she's saying, "Kill me."

D'Souza: I don't think she actually has the right to decide what happens to her body at this point. *Now* the alien is popping out!

Coulter: And the Marines, you'll note, wait until the alien has escaped the womb before burning it with their flamethrowers.

D'Souza: Thereby averting an ethical catastrophe.

Coulter: Here's where Gorman gets Sergeant Apone killed by distracting him. And all hell breaks loose. Look at Gorman's hopeless bungling. "Get them out of there!" Ripley begs him. Gorman is so unnerved by real combat that he can't speak. This silence is well known to any liberal once he has had his fancy little world of pleasant unreality shattered.

D'Souza: Indecision. Lack of resolution. Liberals are terrified by reality.

Coulter: "Do something," Ripley says, throttling Gorman. I love that woman!

D'Souza: And she stuffs Newt in the child seat before she drives in to save the stranded Corporation Marines.

Coulter: And Newt takes off the seatbelt! Some Big Brother directive, like seatbelt-wearing—what good does it do her? She's survived for weeks among liberal aliens. Seatbelts? Please.

Gorman, of course, is knocked unconscious by Ripley's fearless driving. And look at him, the coward. Hit in the head with falling luggage. It's a good thing Bill Clinton *did* dodge the draft. Otherwise he would have led his platoon into some rice-patty disaster much like this one.

D'Souza: Wow. Ripley's run over an alien with the Corporation's armored vehicle.

Coulter: Some *wonderful* alien-killing here. I just like seeing them die. Remember that aliens have acid for blood. They use their own death as a way to kill. Anything that has acid for blood is simply not to be trusted. You can't even kill it without hurting yourself. How is that fair? But they escape. Hicks is telling Ripley they're clear. Where's Gorman? Unconscious, of course.

D'Souza: And in this discussion afterward about whether or not to destroy the entire infested planet, Burke sensibly brings up the fact that the colony has substantial dollar value attached to it.

Coulter: Now, the soldiers have less tolerance for this position.

D'Souza: We honor the soldiers, and we respect them. But they need leaders to tell them what to do. They're six weeks of boot camp away from blowing their welfare checks in a pool hall. Only the imposition of rigid discipline makes them the wonderful servants for democracy that they are.

Coulter: And here we see Ferro killed by a cowardly liberal alien.

D'Souza: Gosh. How did it get up there?

Coulter: I don't know. But they're in a bit of a bind now, especially after Ferro's ship crashes and nearly kills all of them. These aliens may be smarter than they look.

D'Souza: "Game over," says Hudson. Another self-defeating, anti-Corporation coward. Now Burke is suggesting they build a fire and sing some songs. You know, that's not a bad idea.

Coulter: All that's left for them to do now is tally their guns and ammo. Unfortunately, they're low on ammo. Liberals obviously planned this mission. But I bet Gorman packed the ship with alien food aid. Look at this. Newt is showing a natural curiosity for automatic weapons, but Hicks wisely tells her not to touch. Not until she's older, at least. Maybe the flamethrower when she's twelve and the grenade launchers when she's fifteen.

D'Souza: Morale is crumbling here. Hudson cravenly asks, "Why don't you put *her* in charge?" when it's pointed out that Newt has survived among aliens. What are the differences between them? Newt is totally self-reliant. Hudson wants someone to come and save him. He's even willing to rely on a child.

Coulter: And he was the one talking the biggest game in the beginning of the film, as I remember.

D'Souza: So, there's nobody up in the big orbiting ship?

Coulter: It seems no one was left up in the big orbiting ship. That does seem to be another flaw in their tactical plan. I'm pleased, however, to see that the colony relied on fusion, that nuclear power is still a vital part of human society.

D'Souza: Liberals would have insisted on powering everything on the planet with windmills and sunlight, no doubt.

Coulter: And just *look* at Ripley's self-reliant spirit here as she goes about preparing barricades to keep the liberal aliens out. This is sensible Corporation policy. Sealing off whatever doors you have to seal off to keep these things out. This is no place to address the niceties of discriminating against aliens.

D'Souza: Yes. We have to see this as a group of people quite simply *besieged* by aliens. Encircled, as it were, by hostility itself.

Coulter: Hostility that evidences itself by the fact that all these aliens speak a language I don't understand.

D'Souza: This is an appropriate response, of course. What we're seeing is a clash of civilizations: Corporate Earth culture versus alien-insect acid-blood culture.

Coulter: What do you think about the conflict between the always-dapper Burke and the all-American Hicks? It's obvious by this point that they don't like each other.

D'Souza: A lack of mutual understanding, I would say. Burke's a member of the thinking class. He has the bigger picture in mind.

Coulter: Yes, he does. Hicks seems to be the kind of guy who would watch NASCAR, if they still have NASCAR, if the precious alien liberals haven't outlawed it.

D'Souza: And that's great. We need people like Hicks.

Coulter: We *do* need people like that. But fundamentally Burke should be in charge. Now we're coming up on the scene where the face-hugger tries to kill Ripley and Newt in the medi-lab. The movie suggests that Burke released this face-hugger from its tube.

D'Souza: Naturally. He wanted to incubate Newt and Ripley.

Coulter: I will proceed from the assumption that Burke has more faith in the medical industry back home on Earth than any of these grunts. I imagine that Burke knows of some established medical process able to remove the unborn aliens from Newt and Ripley without killing them.

D'Souza: I don't think there's enough information to make a judgment. Again, though, Burke doesn't want to destroy anything that could provide humans with a possible military edge. Such as the aforementioned alien-insect acid blood.

Coulter: As he's explaining to Ripley right now, "We can both come out of this as heroes." In other words, we can use the face-huggers for the good of the Corporation.

D'Souza: Why would anyone simply want to throw away this acid-blood edge?

Coulter: How do you view the revelation that Burke sent the colonists to their deaths? I think Ripley, essentially, likes and respects Burke.

D'Souza: I don't know. I think you're letting your affection for Ripley interfere a little bit with understanding the complexities and nuances of her dilemma. There's more than a little bit of shrill, liberal cant coming out of her mouth at this point.

Coulter: I disagree. I think in the vast tent of conservative thought there's room for pro-alien-annihilation views as well as pro-Corporation views. I also think… wait, what's going on? Oh. I guess this is another new scene cut from the theatrical release.

D'Souza: Yes. We see aliens sneaking through, penetrating the inadequately protected borders, despite the fact that there are two very powerful, well-armed sentry guns and a pressure door between them and the humans. But it doesn't seem to be enough.

Coulter: And now the "artificial person" Bishop points out that a forty-megaton explosion is going to await them all if they don't get off the planet. Hudson, of course, instantly despairs. I think Hudson's incessant cowardice is a dark blight on this otherwise excellent movie. But back to Burke and Ripley. There's room for disagreement within conservatism. Yes, Burke is probably too pro-face-hugger. I can admit that.

D'Souza: Are you advocating nuance and complexity?

Coulter: No. God, no. I'm just saying that if there's a buck to be made off face-huggers, then it should be looked into seriously. And here we see that the sentry guns, which they think are going to fail, ultimately *do* stop the aliens—proving, once again, that guns work.

D'Souza: It also proves that the Corporation should invest even more vigorously in military hardware.

Coulter: In sentry-gun technology. Can you imagine if every American family had a sentry gun in its doorway?

D'Souza: Dare to dream.

Coulter: Here Hicks and Ripley share a quiet moment. Do you find this scene erotic? Hicks teaching Ripley how to shoot the plasma rifle?

D'Souza: I don't know. I'm uncomfortable with eroticism.

Coulter: "Show me everything," Ripley says, "even the grenade launcher." That's a very erotic line to me. Now Ripley, fresh from having learned how to wield a weapon, goes to Newt. We find little feral Newt sleeping under her bed. Wouldn't you say Newt is reminiscent here of Mowgli from *Tarzan*?

D'Souza: From *Tarzan*?

Coulter: *Greystoke*. Whatever it's called. So, Newt and now Ripley are sleeping under the bed and the liberal face-hugger scampers into the room, very nearly impregnating them both. As we've discussed, face-hugging raises complicated issues for conservatism.

D'Souza: We can agree on this: In his concern, in his corporate spirit, Burke is probably taking things a bit too far. But he does so with inimitable style and joie de vivre.

Coulter: They said Ronald Reagan went too far. They always say conservatives are going too far. Liberals never go too far. For liberals, your heart has to be in the right place.

D'Souza: They never go far *enough*.

Coulter: But it doesn't matter if your heart's in the right place if you're going to burn in hell, which is what most liberals are going to do. Perhaps Burke made a mistake. Here he is turning off the security camera—unfortunately while Ripley, menaced by the liberal face-hugger, is frantically waving for help.

D'Souza: Fairly damning evidence. But the circle of self-interest has closed now, as it often does. We're seeing a regrettable but unchangeable aspect of human nature.

Coulter: I'm not certain it's ever totally established that Burke actually *saw* Ripley on the screen there.

D'Souza: It doesn't matter, in the end. If the Corporation has a few bad apples in it—and Burke may or may not be a bad apple—it will nevertheless survive this potentially embarrassing episode.

Coulter: It really doesn't matter, because Ripley triggers the fire detector with her lighter and summons the Marines. Thank God. And *finally*, Hudson reclaims some of his soldierly manhood by wasting the face-hugger.

D'Souza: And now they question Burke.

Coulter: Look, Burke made a mistake. Still, there's no reason to call him a "rat-fuck son of a bitch," like Hudson just did. Hudson, who's gone through about seven diapers since this mission began. Burke, however, has been a picture of calm.

D'Souza: And what does Burke say?

Coulter: Burke says it's "nuts" to accuse him. That they're all suffering from a sad and a paranoid delusion. Personally, I think there may be something to that. Before they all agree to make up and fight for the main and subsidiary interests of the Corporation, the lights go out. And what do we do here? What conclusions do we draw? Were they not vigilant enough about the aliens? Did they not hate them enough? They hated them enough. They were vigilant. But the liberal aliens still got through.

D'Souza: It's an unrelenting tide.

Coulter: If I may go on a bit here and address some metaphorical implications: You'll notice that liberals try to suppress all conservative thought. Why do they do this? Because conservative thought is so much more innately appealing than liberal thought. What I'm saying is that we might draw from this sequence an opposite analogy—that conservatism will always win, it will get through.

D'Souza: Conservative aliens?

Coulter: No, humans fighting for the right and true philosophy. An anti-alien philosophy. The point is relentlessness. We could learn something from these liberal aliens. Note, too, how the aliens get in. Do you recall? The basement and the ceiling. All the hidden places. You can't deal with these creatures head-on.

D'Souza: This is a terrifying scene.

Coulter: They're getting closer.

D'Souza: Now they're inside the room.

Coulter: Those ceilings caved in rather quickly, didn't they? Were these ceiling panels laid by some terra-forming union? Gorman is shooting aliens, but look at the confusion on his face. He's probably still trying to understand them.

D'Souza: Burke runs out here, but we don't really know why. It's possible he was running to get a rifle.

Coulter: This may be my favorite scene: Hudson slaughtering aliens. He's seeing that interspecies genocide, under the proper circumstances, can be invigorating. Hudson has changed.

D'Souza: Well, you know what a conservative is, right? A conservative is a liberal who's been attacked by aliens.

Coulter: This is sad when Hudson dies. Pulled into the depths.

D'Souza: Bravely fighting, though.

Coulter: Would you rather be shot or would you rather be impregnated by an alien?

D'Souza: Well—

Coulter: Again we see Burke running away. And, tragically, he runs into one of the aliens and is killed. Frankly, I begin to lose interest here. It's not the same film without him.

D'Souza: Private Vasquez dies, too, yes?

Coulter: She and Gorman die together. Fitting, in that Gorman is the Clinton-esque figure who dies with a woman in his arms.

D'Souza: He does redeem himself at the end.

Coulter: Gorman?

D'Souza: Yes.

Coulter: By killing. With his little pistol. But what does he *really* do? He goes back to save a Marine who was obviously already going to die, then blows himself and her up—killing a few liberal aliens, I admit—but also sending a fireball through the vents that knocks Newt into the deeper recesses of the complex, separating her from Ripley. It just goes to show you. Even when liberals like Gorman finally do something good, they actually ruin everything.

D'Souza: The road to hell is paved with liberal good intentions.

Coulter: What a genius move by Gorman. Gorman probably would have just left Newt down there.

D'Souza: Or he would have lobbed a few cruise missiles at her and called it a day.

Coulter: After fondling her.

D'Souza: Now, Ann!

Coulter: He would have fondled Newt first! You know he would.

D'Souza: Ripley decides to go back and save the captured Newt. What do we learn? I think we learn that conservatives don't quit. Liberals quit. Again and again through history, they quit. The Soviet Union, most famously.

Coulter: Single-handedly defeated by the magnificent leadership of Ronald Reagan.

D'Souza: Ripley is loading up with ammunition. Takes your breath away, doesn't it?

Coulter: Yes, definitely.

D'Souza: I'm somewhat troubled, though, by Ripley's braless sixties chic.

Coulter: Considering her circumstances, I'm not all that bothered by it. But typically I would like to see her in a bra. And here we are in the aliens' liberal lair. Look at how packed together these aliens are! And that's a big birth canal the mother alien has, isn't it? I mean, it's so big you almost want to give it food stamps.

D'Souza: You're right. She pumps out children like there's no tomorrow and feeds them the corpses of the hard-working, gainfully employed colonists. This is a liberal paradise, evidently.

Coulter: And meanwhile the aliens haven't contributed any technological developments at all. Everything modern on this planet was put here by the colonizers. For that imbalance alone the aliens deserve to be wiped out.

D'Souza: They're basically parasites.

Coulter: They're parasites! And this mother alien just giving *birth* all day. Ripley's got it right when she realizes that destroying the welfare-mother alien is her only option.

D'Souza: With a flamethrower. A flamethrower, moreover, that most liberals will tell you Ripley should not lawfully be able to wield.

Coulter: That's right. She duct-tapes that flamethrower to the plasma rifle, right?

D'Souza: And then she begins shooting those grenades into the welfare queen's egg sac.

Coulter: The mother alien, to save herself from burning to death, pulls free of her uterus and lets all her babies burn to death. What does *that* remind you of? Actually, I don't know what that reminds me of, but it's bad for liberals, whatever it is. Now, did you think the android—I'm sorry, the *artificial person*—was really going to abandon Ripley and Newt here on the catwalk while the complex burns and explodes all around them?

D'Souza: Bishop is a machine. It's going to do what the Corporation tells it to do. At the beginning, it does seem like it's been programmed with some kind of political-correctness chip.

Coulter: Well, he hadn't been attacked by aliens yet.

D'Souza: But now he *has* been attacked by aliens. So it does change everything, doesn't it?

Coulter: Do you think nuclear power is getting a bad rap here due to the fact that it's about to destroy the entire planet?

D'Souza: Well, no, since destroying the whole planet is a necessary course at this point.

Coulter: You see that the aliens have caused all these problems, and, naturally, liberals would want to blame it all on nuclear power and on Burke. For liberals, the main thing is not, "Let's try to win arguments"; it's destroying their opponents by maligning their reputations and, when that fails, leading them into corridors known to be traveled by their hungry alien brethren.

D'Souza: Liberals want to operate in perpetual alarmist mode. They routinely exaggerate the threat that economic growth, technology, and human beings themselves pose to the planet.

Coulter: When it's really aliens that are the problem.

D'Souza: Along with the human beings who have been impregnated by the alien ideology.

Coulter: The music in this escape sequence sounds very much like Wagner's *The Planets*, specifically the first movement.

D'Souza: Boom! The planet explodes. That solved their alien problem, didn't it?

Coulter: It did.

D'Souza: A nice, big, nuclear cloud. Pretty.

Coulter: When your problems are all concentrated in one area, that cloud can be a wonderful problem-solver. But the freeloading welfare queen has stowed away in the escape ship like a common hobo. You think they've escaped. But they have not. And now Bishop gets impaled by her gigantic alien tail. Ugh, milk vomit.

D'Souza: Bishop's milk vomit.

Coulter: I miss Burke.

D'Souza: Notice what this movie didn't have: compassion, understanding, empathy, kindness. Instead we see brute human instinct working for self-preservation.

Coulter: The airlock opens, and good riddance to bad aliens! Not that there's such a thing as *good* aliens.

D'Souza: Well, except perhaps for me.

STAR TREK II:
THE WRATH OF KHAN

[TREKKER MAIL-ORDER EDITION DVD]

Commentary by Terry Dwibble and Steven McCray

Recorded February 2002

TERRY DWIBBLE: Hello. My name is Terry Dwibble.

STEVEN MCCRAY: And I'm Steven McCray.

Dwibble: And we were approached by Rick Berman, current executive producer of *Star Trek*, to contribute our commentary to this special fans-only edition of *Star Trek II: The Wrath of Khan*.

McCray: And what an honor for us. It was thrilling to get the call, because they don't usually do these kinds of things for the fans.

Dwibble: I think before we continue, we should give our credentials. Steven and I are here as Michigan's two biggest supporters of *Star Trek*. I run the largest Captain Clark Terrell fansite—definitely in North America, possibly the world.

McCray: There's that guy in Holland who's got a really great site.

Dwibble: It's a good site, but it doesn't have anywhere near the links that I have.

McCray: Not to mention the fan fiction.

Dwibble: You said it. Steven has generously left more posts on Clarkterrell.com than any other *Star Trek* fan.

McCray: It's always a pleasure. You've bought more than your fair share of memorabilia from my online store, which—don't want to brag—has landed me quite a bit of money here in Kalamazoo.

Dwibble: For other fans out there, you may recognize me as my Net identity: First Officer Narg of the *IKS Gorkon*, which is a Qang-class starship, and veteran of the Dominion War.

McCray: Yeah, we ought to point out that were are going to be referring to ourselves by our *Star Trek* identities. Mine is Lieutenant Commander Tarek of the *U.S.S. Gandhi*, also known as Federation Starship NCC-26632. *Star Trek* has been a big part of our lives, and these identities put us in touch with *Star Trek* fans around the globe and reflect a lifetime of love.

Dwibble: Tarek, we have to keep it down because my wife, my... female, who unfortunately doesn't love *Star Trek* quite as much as I do, is upstairs and if she hears us recording this commentary—

McCray: Didn't you tell her it's for Rick Berman? Does she know how important this is?

Dwibble: She does, but still—

McCray: I think the movie's starting now.

Dwibble: Oh, yes, the movie has started.

McCray: Okay. This is the greatest *Star Trek* movie ever made. You're going to hear a lot of people talk about the different ships and the different casts of *Star Trek*, but as a man in his late 40s, I believe the original crew is still the best. This has been said a million times before. And everybody watching knows it's true.

Dwibble: We open in the midst of Saavik's Kobayashi Maru test.

McCray: This is part of the Starfleet training program that every Federation captain has to go through. This test presents the taker with a no-win scenario. It's a very important part of the thematic structure of this movie and the various things it's exploring about age and mortality, and about how you deal with your own mortality as you get older.

Dwibble: I've always admired the Kobayashi Maru sequence, especially the fact that even though this is the twenty-third century, Starfleet still relies on real explosions on the simulation deck rather than the less-violent holographic display.

McCray: Now, you dealt with this in your own fan fiction in that one novel that you wrote about the lieutenant—

Dwibble: Yes, the young lieutenant who was injured when the simulation went awry. His control panel exploded, and his arm caught on fire. It was a very long novel, but, unfortunately, Pocket Books won't give me the time of day.

McCray: Now that's really the jackpot, though, if you can get something published by Pocket Books.

Dwibble: Yeah, well, I know I'm not a Keith R.A. DeCandido or anybody, but I think I have something to say with my work.

McCray: That guy is a genius.

Dwibble: And here is Admiral Kirk's first appearance.

McCray: He's looking fit. You know people give Shatner a hard time about the girdle, but I think it works for him.

Dwibble: Now, we saw this movie for the first time together.

McCray: Yeah, I remember that. We went on opening night, and you were wearing that great Captain Terrell outfit. I mean, who would have known about Captain Terrell before the movie came out, except you? You knew.

Dwibble: Thanks, Tarek. Now here, Bones is visiting Kirk in his San Francisco apartment.

McCray: Which is where the Federation is located.

Dwibble: He's drinking Romulan ale. I've always admired the Romulans for their ale-making. They may be murderous, but—

McCray: Did you have that Romulan ale that those guys brought to that convention in Indianapolis last winter?

Dwibble: I did. But I think that was just Windex.

McCray: Sure tasted like it. But, I mean, look at Kirk's face when he has a sip. It looks like he's drinking Windex, too.

Dwibble: And here we have Captain Terrell's ship, the *U.S.S. Reliant*. This is the first time we see it, and it's a fine ship.

McCray: There's Captain Terrell looking very commanding.

Dwibble: He's a great captain. My fifth novel, called *Terrell's Gambit*, was sort of a pre-Khan adventure in which he had snuck deep into the Romulan neutral zone.

McCray: Right. And something was wrong with the warp drive.

Dwibble: Well, they had that problem with the dilithium crystals, and then they needed to get new ones.

McCray: I've always wondered, why doesn't the Federation pack more dilithium crystals on their ships? Anyway, I remember reading the book when you sent it over to me. It looked like everyone was going to die and then, miraculously, they pulled through it.

Dwibble: Yeah, the engines were overloaded, and Scotty just happened to be visiting. It was a nod to the classics. Now, we meet Kirk's ex-wife, Dr. Carol Marcus, and their son, David Marcus.

McCray: Ph.D.

Dwibble: Yes. You were rather cruelly cheated out of your Ph.D.

McCray: Yeah, I don't think that's relevant for this commentary.

Dwibble: Well, it's cast a pretty long shadow over your adult life. I know you've always sort of resented me for having mine. But, you know, we don't need to talk about that.

McCray: No, we don't. Let's go back to the movie.

Dwibble: Sure.

McCray: All right, we're beaming down on a planet they think is Ceti Alpha VI but it is actually a Ceti Alpha V. I don't think we're giving away any plot points here.

Dwibble: No, I don't think so. Terrell and Chekov here—

McCray: Remember the anticipation you felt here when you knew that Chekov and Terrell were walking into the hands of Khan?

Dwibble: Only an idiot wouldn't have been able to see it coming.

McCray: Now we're going to go into the *Botany Bay*. Chekov for some reason doesn't recognize this as a Federation cargo vessel.

Dwibble: Well, it's a sandstorm and Chekov is not superhuman.

McCray: True. You know, the *Botany Bay* looks a bit like my basement apartment. And now we have a glorious entrance by Khan, played by Ricardo Montalban, which is just incredible casting.

Dwibble: Unbelievable casting. This is a performance that's up there with, oh gosh, Persis Khambatta or Jeri Ryan.

McCray: He's one of those figures who are unforgettable.

Dwibble: Now a lot of people think that Captain Terrell is not a good captain because of what happens here—

McCray: Because he seems to be behaving like a coward.

Dwibble: Well, Khan is terrifying. I mean, wouldn't you be terrified of Khan? He comes in, he pulls off one glove, bares his obscenely large chest—he's a very sinister guy. And he's got all these Nordic, genetically superior helpers with him.

McCray: And Khan's just devastated to learn that Captain Kirk is actually an admiral now. You know, Khan, too, faces an existential crisis in this movie. He's been marooned on this planet and lost his strongest, best days. It's sad, isn't it?

Dwibble: Well, I've been thinking about that a lot lately myself. You know, my wife and I are no longer sleeping in the same room.

McCray: The guest bedroom is your own little Ceti Alpha V, isn't it?

Dwibble: It is. A little bit. But, you know, I've been thinking about my own contributions to the life that I've had, and I feel good about the twenty-three novels I've written, and the Captain Terrell fansite, and, you know, that I did engage James Doohan for more than three minutes at the 1994 *Star Trek* convention.

McCray: I was there. He was really interested in what you guys were talking about.

Dwibble: He was.

McCray: Not to keep off the movie, but I never understood your marriage.

Dwibble: I know. My female just doesn't understand our world. Now, there was this woman, before my wife, who wanted to go out on a date, but you and I went to see *Undiscovered Country* instead. That was really a great night. I don't remember what we did after, but it was really fun. She got married last year.

McCray: Really?

Dwibble: Yeah, she married a *Star Wars* fan.

McCray: Well, you dodged a bullet there, didn't you?

Dwibble: You bet.

McCray: Look, crash at my place, man. Don't sleep in that guest bedroom. I've got a futon. We could catch up. We could watch all the movies again. Whatever. Just think about it.

Dwibble: Now, Chekov and Terrell are forced to their knees.

McCray: Khan is just casually dropping the mind-altering spawn of this horrible armadillo creature into their helmets.

Dwibble: And now, Kirk, Uhura, Sulu, and Bones are all going back to the *Enterprise*. Can I say something? Is this movie doing it for you anymore? I have to say, I'm a little bored.

McCray: You're *bored*? Why are you bored? This is the best *Star Trek* movie ever made. You're just distracted by all these other things that are happening in your life. You're not thinking clearly. It's like when Saavik says, "*Ish'veh ni homen*," which as we all know is Vulcan for "He's so human."

Dwibble: Or, as we might say in Klingon, "*GhaH Baktag*!"

McCray: That's the spirit. I remember the last time you said that, you scared away a girl at the bar.

Dwibble: Yeah, but, Steve, I'm just thinking maybe—

McCray: My name is not Steve. My name is Tarek.

Dwibble: Right. And I'm Narg. Right.

McCray: Back into character, man.

Dwibble: So, Kirk and Scotty talk— Look, I just can't do it.

McCray: Hey, we're watching *Khan*, man. Just stick to *Khan*.

Dwibble: My wife and I are going to counseling, and the counselor has addressed the fact that maybe you are the problem.

McCray: Wait, what? *I'm* the problem?

Dwibble: Well, remember when the Saavik statues I bought from you? There was this episode where my wife caught me with the Saavik statue... I don't even want to get into that.

McCray: I feel like I'm Spock arguing with Bones right now. You know? Or maybe this is your Klingon temper coming out, but this isn't the time or place. We should just get back to the movie.

Dwibble: Fine. What's happening? I can't even really—

McCray: The *Enterprise* is leaving its moorings.

Dwibble: Yeah, they're going out… and Chekov and Terrell are—

McCray: To this great James Horner score.

Dwibble: Ste— Tarek, do you realize that I haven't updated the Terrell fansite in six months?

McCray: But what about all the things that Terrell's been doing?

Dwibble: They don't seem to matter anymore. I've written twenty-three novels! And none of them have been published. I'm starting to think it's never going to happen for me. That I'm going to be forever overshadowed, a Captain Decker to Keith R.A. DeCandido's Kirk.

McCray: Look, look! We've got the Genesis Project going on. And Khan's taking over the *Reliant*.

Dwibble: And Chekov is under the control of Khan's mind controlling, eel-armadillo creature. And he's luring Carol Marcus and David to Ceti Alpha V. He's going to steal the Genesis Project and use it to take over the universe.

McCray: You know, I'm really into the Starfleet regulation sideburns in this movie. They're shaped like Florida.

Dwibble: I like them too. And Khan's hair looks like the wig Linda Evans wore on *Dynasty*.

McCray: "It's not logical."

Dwibble: That's what Saavik tells Kirk in the elevator. Now, here is Carol Marcus getting in touch with Kirk, but it's breaking up because of some sort of nebular asteroid storm.

McCray: Yeah, there's a photonic disturbance.

Dwibble: So, Kirk is finally alerted to his ex-wife's ordeal here—

McCray: Are you guys going to get divorced?

Dwibble: I don't know. You know, it's been talked about. The estate, such as it is, is hers mostly. All I have is my memorabilia.

McCray: I think you need to listen to the movie, man. This movie is about not being tied down. It's about Kirk making the right decision, early in his life, not to settle down with Carol and raise his son. And he expresses regret, but would we have had all the great *Star Trek* adventures without that?

Dwibble: Just because you didn't get married doesn't give you any right to criticize me. You chose to marry Starfleet. Fine. I can only hear you say that so many times before I feel like you're attacking me.

McCray: It's about commitment, man. It's about commitment.

Dwibble: Here we have Kirk going into Spock's office, and Spock has these beads hanging.

McCray: He's doing his Vulcan meditations. I do them every day.

Dwibble: How's that worked for you?

McCray: It's been great. It's given me great peace of mind.

Dwibble: Despite the fact that you're—

McCray: I don't worry about that stuff. Don't even bring it up. Don't even try to kill my Vulcan harmony.

Dwibble: I was wondering... Can Paramount... Do they have any influence at Pocket Books? Because I'd really like to speak with Keith R.A. DeCandido's editor.

McCray: Yeah, well, I think something can be worked out. Now we're going to see a spectacular bit of early computer-generated special effects. First, Kirk goes through a retinal scan, which I don't think we'd seen outside of a James Bond movie at this point.

Dwibble: No, probably not. Now they're watching Carol Marcus's Federation proposal for Project Genesis, which, as I understand it, is this incredibly powerful force.

McCray: You know about Genesis. Come on! It's implanted on a lifeless planet, and after detonation it allows the planet to breed life. Hence the name Genesis.

Dwibble: Did they name it after Phil Collins's group, Genesis?

McCray: No, it's *not* named after Phil Collins's group, Genesis.

Dwibble: Huh.

McCray: But it does destroy whatever life exists before in favor of its new matrix, as Spock so eloquently puts it.

Dwibble: They're watching the reformed moon that is now a forested, water-based planet, thanks to the Genesis effect. I really feel that my own life could use the equivalent of a Genesis effect. It hasn't been the same since—

McCray: Bones, in his typical hysterical fashion here, is decrying the new technology. It's not logical.

Dwibble: I used to really admire Captain Terrell for his courage and his strength. But now I think he's just kind of a coward.

McCray: Look, this happens to everybody, you know… you lose faith in Roddenberry's vision. But stick with it. And don't confuse your feelings about *Star Trek* with the turmoil caused by your crumbling marriage. I mean, you're all mixed up inside. You need to focus your energy and your intelligence on logical things.

Dwibble: The First Officer Narg part of me is delighted by the *Reliance*'s approach of the *Enterprise* here. Khan is about to shoot some proton torpedoes. I can really feel the tension.

McCray: War! Yes!

Dwibble: The Terry Dwibble part of me, I have to say, Steve, is a sad, scared, little boy.

McCray: You can't live a divided life. Right now I see a good Terry Dwibble and an evil Terry Dwibble. Just like in "The Enemy Within." And you know the evil Terry Dwibble with the goatee? You need to send him back into his own dimension. So, here comes the great confrontation between Kirk and Khan.

Dwibble: Admiral Kirk leaves his shields down way too long here. I've never been able to understand that blunder.

McCray: Bait and switch, man. Bait and switch!

Dwibble: It *is* a Starfleet ship, and I understand that his reluctance to put up the shields for the *U.S.S Reliant* is a mark of respect for Starfleet. But, he had to have sensed something was wrong.

McCray: Well, he was trying to—

Dwibble: Does Joachim seem slightly half-hearted to you in his service of Khan?

McCray: Yeah, I'm feeling, you know, you would understand the Joachim character really well right now.

Dwibble: Steve, you—

McCray: Tarek.

Dwibble: Sorry, Tarek.

McCray: Narg, have you forgotten the moral of this story?

Dwibble: Which is?

McCray: Kirk feels old. Kirk feels like he's going to die. Kirk feels like his best years are behind him. But they're not, man, they're ahead of him. You're just like Kirk in this movie.

Dwibble: Does that make my wife Khan, then?

McCray: I'm not sure what is makes her. Your wife is more like, you know, Carol Marcus. But not as smart. Or as pretty.

Dwibble: Well, she's put on some weight, but you know—

McCray: And what you are is Kirk who got married and works some middle-management job at Starfleet, safe at home. We used to jet all over the country going to *Star Trek* conventions. Visiting all sorts of different planets, meeting all sorts of different aliens.

Dwibble: Remember how offended they were at the Inglewood Con when I donned black face to look like Captain Terrell?

McCray: I didn't understand that.

Dwibble: I'm trying to be the character. Obviously, you have to wear black shoe polish all over your face. I mean, what is so illogical about that? Those people freaked out.

McCray: Um, let's get back to the movie.

Dwibble: Now, we have Khan and Kirk facing off. Khan attacks the *Enterprise*. Kirk's shirt is unbuttoned. He puts his glasses on. Now Khan's ship is hit by Kirk. Are you really still into this? The special effects there with the smoke coming out of the thing is pretty cheesy. And the Linda Evans wig that Khan is wearing is pretty hard for me to overlook now.

McCray: Well, okay, but—

Dwibble: And have you ever wondered why Scotty dragged the corpse of his burned nephew up to the bridge of the *Enterprise?*

McCray: It *is* illogical to bring a wounded officer up to the bridge.

Dwibble: "Is the word given, Captain?" That's what Preston says to Kirk. Kirk says, "Warp speed." And then he dies.

McCray: How many times did you cry when you watched this movie? This movie was a three-cry for me.

Dwibble: It was a four-cry for me.

McCray: Really?

Dwibble: Yeah. "He stayed at his post. When the trainees ran, he stayed at his post." That's Scotty talking about Preston. You know, I'm going to stay at my post, Steve.

McCray: I'm glad you're going to stay at your post. That's what I want to hear.

Dwibble: It was the bloody handprint on Kirk's vest that brought me back. It reminded me why I spend seventeen hours a day updating my Captain Terrell fansite. Of course, I haven't done it in six months. That time's been mostly spent at counseling and—

McCray: How's the job search going?

Dwibble: Surprisingly, speaking Klingon is not a skill that's in very wide demand right now.

McCray: You know, if you want to help out at the store—

Dwibble: I don't know. John is there all the time. And I don't like that whole dynamic the two of you have.

McCray: What do you have against Captain Pike?

Dwibble: Well, you two speak in Vulcan. I feel self-conscious. I only know Klingon. You two just seem to be a lot closer. Plus, my wife doesn't want me going. She's said that several times.

McCray: This commentary's going to really help out on the money front, I have a feeling. I mean, I didn't talk terms, but, you know, they have a lot of money over there at Paramount.

Dwibble: So, it looks like we just missed a lot. Kirk, Saavik, and Bones just beamed on to Carol Marcus's research station here.

McCray: This is a terrifying scene. Bones turns and walks into the bloody, hung-up corpse of one of the space station scientists.

Dwibble: That's one of the few bloody, hung-up corpses that you see in the *Star Trek* films.

McCray: This movie might have the most graphic violence in all of the *Star Trek* movies.

Dwibble: I certainly wouldn't let my child watch this if I ever had a child. It's too violent.

McCray: Violent? You think this is more violent than the other movies this child would be watching? Are you going to raise him in a box, this imaginary child of yours?

Dwibble: I don't want him associating *Star Trek* with violence. I want him to associate *Star Trek* with things like rational harmony, interstellar peace, and fighting lizard men on desert planets.

McCray: Terrell's back!

Dwibble: Terrell's back, and he's in hypnosis. Kirk is interrogating him and Chekov about where Carol is.

McCray: Khan really got to him, didn't he?

Dwibble: Terrell's been tortured. He's really been messed with.

McCray: You know, the most brilliant thing you wrote was that one novel, number twenty-two.

Dwibble: I worked hard on that.

McCray: The one about Terrell's captain's log during this period, when he's narrating his ongoing torment by the Ceti eels.

Dwibble: It's my most experimental novel. Pocket held onto it for seven months, which was the longest they held any of my books.

McCray: Maybe you don't need to publish with Pocket Books. Maybe you could publish this yourself.

Dwibble: But that wouldn't have the Roddenberry licensing agreement. I could do whatever I wanted. I could make Kirk a murderer. I could have Spock feeling Mr. Bones's package. And you and I agreed that the fundamental tenet of writing fan fiction was, whether or not we were published, to adhere strictly to all Roddenberry directives.

McCray: You're telling me you don't write unlicensed fan fiction?

Dwibble: No!

McCray: You haven't written any sexual escapades between Kirk and some other species? With Chekov?

Dwibble: Never intended for publication, no!

McCray: Okay, but you wrote them. You've got to check out this new inflatable Saavik that we're selling on the website.

Dwibble: Whoa... is that licensed?

McCray: Not everything has to be licensed, you know. There's a whole black market of *Star Trek* memorabilia.

Dwibble: How many holes does it have?

McCray: I'll show you later.

Dwibble: Is it three? Or the standard two? Because I would be interested in a three-hole Saavik.

McCray: Let's just say Vulcans have slightly different anatomies than humans.

Dwibble: Interesting. Well, I would be all over that inflatable Saavik doll before you could say *megh'an*.

McCray: Yes, well, back to the movie. We're having a real Greek tragedy here. Son fighting father.

Dwibble: What do you think when Kirk realizes that he's just been beating up his son, David, here?

McCray: I think he's thinking David has a really bad hairdo.

Dwibble: You have to be quiet now because Terrell has just betrayed them.

McCray: Chekov, too. This is devastating: Chekov turning a gun on his own captain. Terrell is talking to Khan now. Khan wants to torture Kirk by consigning him to a lifetime buried deep in a lifeless planetoid in space.

Dwibble: But first, Terrell vaporizes one of Marcus's assistants with his phaser.

McCray: See, he has blood on his hands. Maybe that's why Terrell can't live with himself.

Dwibble: He's resisting Khan here. No one else in this movie can resist Khan. Chekov doesn't succeed, but Terrell does.

McCray: Yeah, after Terrell murders an innocent Starfleet scientist.

Dwibble: But now he rips off the wristwatch through which he's speaking to Khan and he bravely vaporizes himself. One of the most moving sequences of all the films.

McCray: Kirk's just vaporized the little insect that's crawled out of Chekov's ear covered with blood.

Dwibble: Yeah, that's exactly what I was talking about earlier.

McCray: All right, maybe, you know, it shouldn't be seen until you're at least 15 human age, 53 Vulcan age.

Dwibble: Now we just heard Kirk famously screaming "Khan... Khan!" into the darkness of space. You really like that, don't you?

McCray: Yes, it's another "Stella" moment in cinematic history.

Dwibble: Here we're at a little downtime in the movie. Khan has taken Genesis, Carol, and David, and Bones, Kirk, and Saavik are all stuck. And, frankly, it's kind of a big drag at this point.

McCray: I'm surprised *you're* not interested in the reconciliation between Kirk and Carol.

Dwibble: It just rings a little hollow right now, to be honest. She asked me to leave, Steve.

McCray: She's asked you to leave?

Dwibble: She told me to get out. I don't really know what to do.

McCray: Well, you know what my counsel is, Narg.

Dwibble: Yeah.

McCray: You were never a well-matched couple. I never quite understood what she saw in you anyway.

Dwibble: Well, she went to Eastern and I went to Central. She thought I was an intellectual, you know. The first love letter I ever wrote her was in Klingon, and she was impressed by that. And then she found out Klingon was a made-up language—

McCray: Can I be brutally honest with you?

Dwibble: Of course.

McCray: Did you guys have any problems with your *Star Trek*, um… passion before you lost your job?

Dwibble: Well, I've maintained that if I could ever put enough effort into it, the Clarkterrell.com fansite, we'll be able to make enough money as long as the PayPal donations keep coming in and please, everyone, keep them coming in. We need them. I've almost broken into the triple figures. I'm very excited about that.

McCray: Here's Phase II of Genesis. Look at how beautiful this is.

Dwibble: If only Paul Winfield would help. I mean, I think that could push me over the edge, you know, with the fans. But he won't even submit to a Q & A. He sent a statement that says he just wishes not to discuss *Star Trek II: The Wrath of Khan* anymore, implying that he gets hundreds of letters about it a year. So, now comes the final face-off between Khan and Kirk. I know, Tarek, you're pretty excited about this. The Narg part of me certainly is, but the Terry part is still suffering, still drifting in the nebula.

McCray: These are some *very* exciting shots: people walking down corridors in the *Enterprise* holding strange lit-up implements.

Dwibble: Now, Tarek, you're sounding a little sarcastic here at the end of *Star Trek II: The Wrath of Khan*. What's going on?

McCray: I'm going bankrupt.

Dwibble: What?

McCray: The website isn't making any money. I basically convinced my friends to buy items—and I thank you for the Saavik statue—but they're not selling outside of the small circle of people I know from the conventions.

Dwibble: But, the Saavik inflatable doll—

McCray: I owe a lot of people money.

Dwibble: Well, I've always forgiven you the fact that you never paid me for those three Birds of Prey.

McCray: I'm just saying, I don't think I can keep this up either.

Dwibble: Do you remember when you yelled at my wife during the picnic? You were there with that woman that you met at the grocery store. And you'd told her that you were a merchandising mogul. She was very angry when she found out you weren't. And you yelled at my wife for telling her the truth. You didn't seem very Vulcan-like then. You seemed explosive and temperamental. It's the only date you've ever been on.

McCray: It's not the only date I've ever been on.

Dwibble: Well, other than John, who have you dated?

McCray: I'm not dating John! John is just a friend. He's like my ward. He lives at my house. He helps me with the store.

Dwibble: Does he know you are going bankrupt?

McCray: He ran away with the money.

Dwibble: John ran away with your money?

McCray: He totally scammed me.

Dwibble: I don't know what to say... other than the fact that for the first time I'm noticing that Khan's crew sort of looks like the guys in *Road Warrior*. Do you know where John is now?

McCray: I'm talking to authorities all through the Midwest. He can't go far. I know his family is from Venice Beach, so I've got some leads. I'm not convinced that he was much of a Trekker.

Dwibble: Learned just enough Vulcan to get by?

McCray: I wanted so much to believe.

Dwibble: Well, there are other wards. I'm sure you'll find one. When's the next convention? Are you going to Milwaukee?

McCray: I don't think I can afford a trip to Milwaukee right now.

Dwibble: I could lend you the $78 I made on PayPal donations.

McCray: I don't need your charity.

Dwibble: You know, Spock has accepted help. He's your idol.

McCray: You know I just wanted say about when I yelled at the picnic, and I'm really sorry I yelled like that and I lost my cool, but I was going through a tough time and I didn't have control of myself.

Dwibble: Well, I understand that.

McCray: I mean, it's not often that I get a chance to even be with a woman and the prospect of having sex really brings out this kind of emotion.

Dwibble: I told you, *Star Trek* is wonderful, but there are moments, sex being one of them, where *Star Trek* is not an appropriate worldview through which to approach life experience, you know? It's not just handing an orb back and forth to each other. You actually really have to become naked with someone.

McCray: This coming from the man with the failed marriage.

Dwibble: My marriage has nothing to with sex. My marriage's problem is that my wife doesn't understand my love of Klingon, my obsession with *Star Trek*. She's never understood that.

McCray: But this movie can help us.

Dwibble: Maybe.

McCray: Now we're having some kind of interstellar dogfight here in a gigantic nebula.

Dwibble: Yeah. It's really pretty boring, actually.

McCray: And another thing: Why do they just have this one TV screen in front of the cockpit? Wouldn't you rather have a wider view? Or have some sort of arrangement whereby you could see in more than one direction?

Dwibble: Yeah, that's a good idea.

McCray: I mean, we seem to be surprised when something swings into view. But they have more than one camera on this ship, don't they?

Dwibble: Scanners, too, I would think. Of course, they would be all rendered powerless in the nebula. This isn't *Battlestar Galactica*, Tarek, so I don't think we can expect the high degree of science-fiction realism that something like Lorne Greene on *Battlestar Galatica* will give you.

McCray: You know, that show's *really* coming back. Now Khan is just about to detonate the Genesis Device. Blah, blah, blah.

Dwibble: I think we're going to have to tell Rick Berman that we need another go at this. This one didn't really work out.

McCray: Here Spock is going to expose himself to lethal radiation.

Dwibble: When Spock is bombarded by gamma rays here why doesn't he turn into, like, a Vulcan Hulk?

McCray: Vulcans are already like Hulks, with the really repressed rage and superhuman strength. They just don't "Hulk out." They walk around as David Banner 99.99 percent of the time.

Dwibble: That's Bruce Banner. David Banner was only in the TV series. They changed Bruce Banner's name to David because television executives feared Bruce was too gay of a name.

McCray: Is that right?

Dwibble: That's true.

McCray: Jesus.

Dwibble: You should ask John about that. He'd probably know. But then, you never saw that in him, did you?

McCray: Saw what?

Dwibble: That's what I thought.

McCray: Spock's really got his face over that stream of radiation.

Dwibble: Yeah.

McCray: That's got to hurt.

Dwibble: Well, he's a Vulcan. So, it's not of the same—

McCray: Don't tell me about Vulcans. I know about Vulcans.

Dwibble: I know you know.

McCray: I'm just saying. Vulcans hurt. Even Vulcans cry, all right. If you prick us, do we not bleed? If you expose us to extraordinarily high levels of radiation, do our faces not peel off?

Dwibble: In Klingon there's a similar saying, but they say, "If you beat my face to a bloody pulp with a pipe, do we not roar?"

McCray: All right. Khan's got a really bloody face right now. He's gloating as the *Enterprise* tries to flee.

Dwibble: We should probably talk about what's happening here. The *Enterprise* can't go to warp speed because it's damaged.

McCray: This is kind of a weak explosion at first. But then we get this great little band of radiation. Oh. Look what's happening.

Dwibble: What's happening?

McCray: Kirk noticed that Spock is gone. Spock's not in his chair.

Dwibble: Yeah. You're really moved by that even after the eighty-third time you've seen this. And, I have to admit, now that I hear James Horner's score, it's getting to me too.

McCray: And when Bones says, "He's dead already," it's like a *taj* in the heart. You know? And you just don't want to believe that he couldn't get out of it.

Dwibble: It's like when you read the Bible, and when Jesus gets killed you're so surprised. You just can't believe that this cool character is being—

McCray: I know. I had never read the Bible until I saw this movie, and I remember thinking, "It's just like Spock. He'll rise again."

Dwibble: I love how Spock straightens his uniform here before he turns to face Kirk with his radiation burned face.

McCray: This is Vulcan grace for you right here.

Dwibble: Until he slams his face into the partition.

McCray: Wait. "Needs of the many outweigh the needs of the few." It's all so clear to me now. Let me ask you a question.

Dwibble: Sure.

McCray: Perhaps the needs of the many *Star Trek* fans, the legions of people at the conventions, and the dozens of people who read your work and faithfully visit your Captain Terrell fansite, maybe their needs outweigh the needs of your selfish wife or your own desire for carnal pleasure.

Dwibble: As you say this, I'm watching Spock die with his horribly radiation-burned face, and I feel the words that you've spoken were not Vulcan words. That was Steve talking to me as a friend, as someone who spent over thirty years enjoying *Star Trek*, who stood by me every time I drafted a new Bird of Prey.

McCray: Why do we always end up crying like this? Come on, give me the Vulcan hand salute. Come on. Let's do it. Come on.

Dwibble: Okay. We've done it. I feel better. I need to make some changes. I need to get my wife out of here. Just because it's her house doesn't mean she can throw me out of it. And you, my friend, need to track John down, and then you need to start selling those inflatable Saavik dolls. Now, here is Spock's funeral.

McCray: Kirk is saying his last words. "He's so human." I'm never quite sure what that means, but I guess it's a positive thing.

Dwibble: And Scotty plays the bagpipes.

McCray: Yes. "Amazing Grace."

Dwibble: I wrote some Klingon songs recently. They're not quite as good as the ones that I got off of Keith R.A. DeCandido's website. There are a lot more instruments in his songs. He has a lot more money. Pocket Books probably pays him pretty well.

McCray: Well, a lot better than nothing.

Dwibble: Thanks, Steve. *Jesus.* You know, it's just the same—

McCray: Oh, come on. Don't you feel reborn right now?

Dwibble: I felt reborn up until you started attacking me again for no reason. My wife is right about you. Wait, I'm sorry I said that. Come on, you can't just sit here and not talk. Rick Berman is going to listen to this.

McCray: I think I'll be going now.

Dwibble: Steve just left. He'll be back. David and Kirk here are having... I guess this is the last scene of the movie. You'd think I'd remember. Well, Steve just walked back in.

McCray: Have you calmed down? Or are you going to "Klingon out" on me again?

Dwibble: No. I'm sorry.

McCray: Want some Cheetos?

Dwibble: Yeah.

PLANET OF THE APES

[LIMITED-EDITION 700 CLUB GOLD MEMBERSHIP BONUS DVD]

Commentary by Jerry Falwell and Pat Robertson

Recorded December 2001

PAT ROBERTSON: Welcome to a very special DVD presentation of *Planet of the Apes*. I'm here with my very good friend and fellow servant of the Lord, Jerry Falwell, and we'll be providing a commentary of sorts on this popular American movie, which neither of us has yet seen.

JERRY FALWELL: That's right, Pat. Though I'm told this is very Christian movie, and it does star my good friend Chuck Heston.

Robertson: Well, let's see what's going on here. We are with a crew of a ship in outer space. And Mr. Heston is making an entry into his diary about his space mission, which has just been completed. They are about to put themselves in deep sleep for the long ride back to Earth.

Falwell: I notice that Heston is applying a syringe to himself, and I don't know what that's about, but I hope that he is complying with—uh—well, I'm sure he is—maybe he's a diabetic.

Robertson: I think what he's doing is preparing himself for the deep sleep that he's about to enter into.

Falwell: I didn't realize there was a woman on the spaceship.

Robertson: Yes, there are four people on the spaceship, four scientists.

Falwell: I disapprove of that, too. I hate to sound like a Puritan.

Robertson: And we have a horrific crash scene here where the spaceship touches down onto this planet.

Falwell: Oh, heavens. The spaceship has crash-landed into what looks like a lake in the middle of a desert.

Robertson: Yes, the spaceship is now floating in water. The astronauts have grown neat beards during their hibernation. And we see Heston with two other men waking from their slumber, not quite sure where they are.

Falwell: I must say that the beards give them a downright apostolic quality.

Robertson: They've discovered that their female companion, the fourth of the scientists, has died in her sleep.

Falwell: And now the water is pouring into the spaceship. As the Lord said unto the apostle Paul: "And now, why are you waiting? Arise and be baptized, and wash away your sins." Amen.

Robertson: And the spaceship is sinking into the lake. Frantic activity in the cabin.

Falwell: Here is an important point. Heston notices that the year is 3978.

Robertson: Which means that almost 2,000 years exactly have passed since they left Earth.

Falwell: Well, I think it's interesting that the same amount of time has passed since the year of our Lord Jesus Christ's birth.

Robertson: Jerry, I have to say the shades of Christian allegory in this movie are striking so far.

Falwell: Well, these men are Americans, you can see. These are astronauts stranded on the rock, and they're Americans—we can tell by the arm patches. They are the new Christian soldiers.

Robertson: Yes. They're clothed in white. We have prominent American flag patches on their arms. We're in a desert environment, which screams "Holy Land" to me.

Falwell: There are three of them, let's not forget.

Robertson: A Trinity. And they've just been baptized in water with their crashing spaceship.

Falwell: And of course Charlton Heston carries his own sort of biblical weight. I must say he's one of the finest interpreters of biblio-filmic art that I know.

Robertson: Yes. Who could forget his work in *The Ten Commandments*? Or *Ben-Hur*? And in a less ecclesiastical vein, I've always loved his work in *El Cid* and *The Agony and the Ecstasy*—

Falwell: He played a homosexual in that one.

Robertson: Michelangelo?

Falwell: Yup. He was gay.

Robertson: I didn't know that. Did you ever see *The Naked Jungle*, when Heston plays a South American plantation owner besieged by killer ants?

Falwell: No.

Robertson: Fantastic.

Falwell: And, of course, he's an important cultural figure, with his work for the NRA. A great American. What's happening in the movie? There seems to be a lot of walking around in the desert.

Robertson: The astronaut-apostles are not sure right now where they are. They had intended to land on Earth, but clearly they are on an abandoned, desolate planet. But for the lack of a woman, we'd have to think of this as a wonderful opportunity to spread the word of God to a new planet.

Falwell: Right. These men are missionaries.

Robertson: Now, we can't ignore the fact that there's a biting cynicism in the Charlton Heston character, Taylor.

Falwell: In a sense he's also a prodigal son, and I think it's important to realize that even though Heston himself is an entirely admirable man, he's not afraid to put himself in roles where he must play the questioner, a tormented soul. He will suffer for it and yet be reborn. "He journeyed to a far country, and there wasted his possessions with prodigal living." So sayeth the Lord.

Robertson: Thanks, Jerry. I'm familiar with the Gospel of Luke. Many people simplify the struggle in the Bible. The Bible is the revelation of God, but enlightenment does not come easy. Charlton Heston's character is, if nothing else, an embodiment of that spiritual struggle. And I believe the movie will bear me out.

Falwell: "But without faith, it is impossible to please Him, for he who comes to God, must believe that He is, and that he is a rewarder of those who—"

Robertson: —diligently seek Him," Hebrews 11:16. I got it, Jerry. Stop showing off. The astronauts continue to cross the desert. Wow. That might be the most thrilling scene of a run down a hill since *Little House on the Prairie*. You know, this movie shows—and I don't see the movies a lot—but there's a lot of fancy special effects and gizmos in movies today, and this movie seems to be doing a lot with straightforward drama and passion.

Falwell: Note the thunder here, as they wander across the barren wilderness.

Robertson: Now, if Heston is the prodigal son, then he went into space to try to discover new things through science, but now returning to Earth he realizes that the revelation of God is the true knowledge and that all of that blasting through space was nothing.

Falwell: God is always with you. Do you know the story of the footprints on the beach? You see—

Robertson: Yes, an inspirational parable, Jerry. Okay, here the Christ-onauts wander through the desert. We're not quite sure how long they've been wandering. This, of course, is again extremely suggestive of a—

Falwell: These men are a tribe.

Robertson: —a tribe wandering through the desert.

Falwell: I must say the movie is a bit slow, even for my taste. I'd like to get to the beasts. And where are these apes? It's taking a good bit of time in the desert.

Robertson: But this is, of course, a part of the struggle. We can't rush this. We have to fully appreciate what it's like to be trapped in the desert without bearings, without any kind of mission.

Falwell: I'm just glad that we're sitting here in a studio and I can get up and have a sandwich.

Robertson: Heston here chides one of his companions as they march through the desert. He's mocking him for his worldly ambitions and the fact that he went into space to become a famous man, to be remembered forever, to achieve immortality. Heston, of course, knows that the only immortality is in accepting Christ as your savior and joining him in the Kingdom after death, and that all of these earthly glories are worth nothing, even if he doesn't say so explicitly.

Falwell: These men are having a hard time here. They're sweating. It's hot. They've escaped boulders and thunderstorms. These are trials. These men are being put through fire.

Robertson: Put through fire, and yet Heston manages to meet it with a certain panache as he smokes a cigar.

Falwell: The astronauts have discovered life in the form of a small shrub—flowers, I guess—a desert rose.

Robertson: Life. There is life in this barren wilderness. Jerry, this movie is called *Planet of the Apes*.

Falwell: That's right, Pat.

Robertson: Um, I haven't seen any apes yet, and I'm really mystified by that.

Falwell: Well, I hope it's not a reference to these men as apes. I know that's something that's very fashionable in liberal scientific circles and think that's a kind of blasphemy, if you'll pardon the expression, against the work of our Lord. We were made with the precious nature of God, in the image of God, by God Himself. For men are beautiful, especially Charlton Heston.

Robertson: Now we're seeing signs of intelligent life. What do you make of those scarecrow-like things on the hilltop?

Falwell: They're cruciform in nature, I must say. Perhaps they've stumbled on a primitive Christian culture.

Robertson: Well, this would make sense because God is the God of all solar systems and other planets. These are definitely crucified figures up on the ledge, and they're going up to explore.

Falwell: Our astronauts seem to have found a kind of desert oasis. Praise the Lord. With water.

Robertson: Yes, the apostles have stumbled upon an Eden in the middle of this desert. Their first reaction to seeing this—the bountiful nature that God has provided them—is to disrobe completely and jump in the water. My, there's quite a bit of nudity in this scene. Fortunately it is only men swimming together.

Falwell: Right, there's no danger of hanky-panky since their female compatriot passed away in the voyage.

Robertson: So this, too, perhaps represents the baptism that we were speaking of earlier. And after emerging from this water is where the symbolic rebirth will be made manifest.

Falwell: These men are washing again and again—oh look—

Robertson: They appear to be—um—

Falwell: I don't—no, no—

Robertson: I'm not sure what to make of that. Heston is standing in his birthday suit right next to the other two nude men, and they both kneeled down next to him off-frame.

Falwell: I think... the better to inspect the human footprint in the mud that they found.

Robertson: Let's hope. I'll stick with that explanation. Now their worldly vestments are taken away from them by these mysterious shadowy figures. They've been literally stripped naked.

Falwell: If we're all naked before God's eyes, these fellows are naked before everyone's. The movie is careful to show these nude men from the waist up, and I think that's a responsible move on the director's part. That's quality directing, Pat.

Robertson: Yes, Jerry. It's very tastefully done. Enough to suggest the nudity. There's absolutely no need to be so graphic about violence and nudity, unless we're looking at the naked Christ nailed to the cross.

Falwell: No, this isn't some degenerate, smutty scene like you'd get in *Boogie Nights* or watching *Teletubbies*.

Robertson: There's nothing worse than being forced to watch those smutty movies in order to protect our congregations from them. It's a task I never look forward to—when I'm forced to vet the latest crop of films that's come out from Hollywood.

Falwell: I truly cringe every time.

Robertson: It takes up a good deal of my time I must say. It really cuts into the preaching. And now their robes have been torn to shreds by these mysterious figures who are running off into the woods. They don't look like apes at all.

Falwell: Oh, well, a wide shot now. They look very primitive. They look like they're in desperate need of a mission.

Robertson: They do. There's an prelapsarian quality to this world, however. But for their crude animal-skin clothing, they could be back in Eden.

Falwell: Pat, right now I would be chomping at the bit to spread the Word to these people if I were in those astronauts' shoes.

Robertson: To start anew. To create a new, pure world. A kingdom based on the worship of Jesus Christ, unmediated by the corrupting influences of culture, other religions, other hedonistic ideas, and pagan beliefs. But now everyone pauses like a herd of animals on the African savanna—they're running. But from what?

Falwell: There was a sound, Pat. A terrible roar.

Robertson: This could be the devil, or some kind of manifestation of the devil, on this planet.

Falwell: I wouldn't put it past this movie to give us an actual physical manifestation of the devil.

Robertson: And through this cornfield, we see large sticks being waved at them, and they're running from the sticks. Ooh... we have horses now. Guns!

Falwell: Guns! I thought we were in a primitive world. Suddenly we're in a technological world. Oh! Oh!

Robertson: My God, what is on top of that horse?

Falwell: They're monkeys. They're gorillas.

Robertson: These must be the apes. Apes riding horses?!

Falwell: And they're dressed in the vestments of humans. It's truly strange.

Robertson: This is indeed a topsy-turvy world.

Falwell: There is something horrible about this enslavement. And yet it is exciting, Pat.

Robertson: It's very exciting. But these humans seem to be no match for the ape creatures riding the horses. And, um, I'm going to have to think about this a little bit, because, while everything's in the Bible, the Bible hasn't prepared me for this.

Falwell: Well, we're clearly in an inverted world where beast holds dominion over man. What the movie's going to teach us from this, I'm not sure yet.

Robertson: Thank God these apostolic saviors have arrived to help lead these humans against the horrific—

Falwell: Oh!

Robertson: One of the astronauts has been shot.

Falwell: We just lost one of our apostles. Apes are shooting men. Men are jumping in a pit.

Robertson: It's a massacre.

Falwell: This is a very violent film. I would say, just as a note to parents, if you're watching this with your children, please take them out of the room now. We should have said that earlier.

Robertson: I think we should have said that when they started stripping down naked and swimming in the water.

Falwell: Well, maybe they can put a note on the box. Do you know what this was rated? Did Heston just get shot?

Robertson: Heston has also been shot and has fallen down. Now we have these horrible apes carrying humans on their back and stringing them up like pieces of meat. And as I see the carts wheeled by with human slaves, I can't help but think there's something of imperial Rome about these—

Falwell: That's exactly the metaphor I was going to use.

Robertson: —about these apes and their culture here. But for the guns, this is a godless, pagan, Roman world. And now Heston is confronted with these human beings who are unaccountably on this planet in the middle of space.

Falwell: Whoa. Monkeys talking. And they've got cameras. They're carrying out this—oh, dear.

Robertson: Heston, captured and shot, has been taken to a monkey village. And the monkeys seem to have a pretty impressive technology... especially for monkeys.

Falwell: It just goes to show that technology isn't good or the work of the Lord. Heston's in some kind of laboratory now. Pat, the monkeys seem to be performing lab experiments on the humans.

Robertson: So it seems. Every ape we've met is either a soldier or a scientist. Dr. Zira is an animal psychologist. And the animals are these people in the cages. I think I'm going to be sick.

Falwell: A Dr. Zaius has appeared. He's a senior scientist in this monkey world.

Robertson: There seem to be different... We have Dr. Zaius wearing an orange leather coat. He looks like an orangutan. There seems to be a hierarchy here. Dr. Zaius serving as some kind of priest in this world. And clearly a priest of a pagan religion. His inability to believe that a human being can speak—clearly the revelation of God has not reached him.

Falwell: How could it? He's an unbaptized monkey in the middle of outer space!

Robertson: Man has no understanding, says Dr. Zaius.

Falwell: Well, that's true if he doesn't know God. Sayeth the Book of John: "Except a man be born again, he cannot see the Kingdom of God."

Robertson: Without the revelation of God, it's true.

Falwell: And in a way, when an inverted person, or a monkey like Dr. Zaius, speaks an inverted truth, the negatives cancel each other out, and it becomes true. Not to put too fine a point on it.

Robertson: I have a grudging respect for this Zaius ape. It's hard to argue too much with his cynicism about the value of science. In a strange way he's on to something, even though he serves a pagan monkey-god. Another accidental truth: He sees no point in the study of man. The proper study of man, of course, not being man but God.

Falwell: One thing that I think is interesting in this right now is Heston's character has been shot in the throat and cannot speak. He cannot communicate the Lord's Word to these apes, but I have to believe that at some point he will be. I hope that he will be able to communicate and be able to preach to them, to testify.

Robertson: Yes, well, if this movie has any—if it's to be saved and become the Christian work that I believe it is, then he will have to be unmuzzled and spread the Gospel.

Falwell: Look… here Heston is trying to communicate. He's still speechless, but he's trying to write in the sand. He's inscribing the very words in the earth. Oh, no—and his—

Robertson: —concubine—

Falwell: —his heathen concubine—is erasing his attempt to spread the Word.

Robertson: This is a sad scene.

Falwell: Heston is fighting with some of his fellow humans.

Robertson: They're only humans in a technical sense. Not having the revelation, they're really not much better than the apes. Violence is regrettable, but according to Scripture, "He is God's servant to do you good. But if you do wrong, be afraid, for he does not bear the sword for nothing. He is God's servant, an agent of wrath to bring punishment on the wrongdoer."

Falwell: And these apes, for all their "civilization," are, without revelation, not much better than nontalking apes.

Robertson: No, they're really only a step above these primitive humans out in the jungle.

Falwell: Barking up the wrong tree, if you will. Or whatever apes do. Do they bark?

Robertson: I think they screech.

Falwell: Oh.

Robertson: Oh, but Dr. Zaius is now seeing the Word of God in the ground… and he scratches it out. Is there any doubt now that Dr. Zaius is a simian Antichrist? Thus, an Antiheston.

Falwell: Yes. He's a man of science who fears the Word, the truth.

Robertson: But isn't that true of so many men of science who are blinded by technical details and facts and data?

Falwell: These are chimeras.

Robertson: There's something about Dr. Zira that is very appealing. Even as Heston grabs her about the head and rips the pen and paper from her meager ape hands—and again Heston experiences humiliation—

Falwell: I almost expect to see a crown of thorns produced.

Robertson: But he's passed a note: "My name is Taylor."

Falwell: A truly humble profession, worthy of a purveyor of God's Word.

Robertson: A carpenter, a tailor—

Falwell: A fisherman—

Robertson: A fisherman. Don't forget the various mongering trades. A carpenter builds things; a tailor makes simple clothing.

Falwell: Taylor's from Fort Wayne, Indiana.

Robertson: It was no doubt in that secular public high school in Indiana that he was infected with this—

Falwell: Secularism.

Robertson: —secularism and cynicism that he will have to be saved from in this movie.

Falwell: Yes, yes. It's interesting how Taylor is both Christ and denier of Christ in one. Complicated.

Robertson: Very complicated. So this is interesting. Zira's monkey-mate, Cornelius, like some kind of simian John the Baptist, foretold the coming of Taylor or, at least, posited the existence of someone like Taylor through his archeological research.

Falwell: Cornelius is referred to as a kind of monkey archaeologist.

Robertson: But also a heretic to the prevailing monkey ideology and religion. These monkeys aren't all bad.

Falwell: Could it be, Pat, that there's some symbolism here? Maybe we shouldn't be reading them strictly as monkeys but as metaphors of the conflict between the Lord and the secular atheists.

Robertson: Well, there's certainly no doubt that every story is about God and Christ and the relationship of man with God. I'm beginning to see clearly here that Dr. Zaius and these orangutan Pharisees—I think we can call them that—are somehow trying to block the revelation that Taylor has brought from the sky.

Falwell: The Word and the Truth are not always easily spoken, especially in these tenuous early stages.

Robertson: But they will always be revealed.

Falwell: Praise the Lord.

Robertson: Hallelujah.

Falwell: Thanks be to you, Lord Jesus Christ.

Robertson: Amen.

Falwell: Dr. Zaius doesn't want to believe anything about Taylor/Heston. The apes want to geld Heston. They want to rob this fine man of his very manhood. Though I can't condone violence, hopefully he'll—

Robertson: Be fruitful and multiply. It's among the first injunctions of God to man, and Heston will not allow that to occur without a fight. And now he's escaped from his pen, and he's running away through this ape city, chased by gorillas.

Falwell: He's adorned in tatters.

Robertson: A frightful sight for these ape heretics to see.

Falwell: Right. Sometimes prophets don't come in neat packages.

Robertson: And now it appears that Heston has walked into a sort of temple, where the apes are worshipping a gigantic ape idol.

Falwell: He flees outside...

Robertson: Like Christ in the temple, he's tearing apart this city and all of its decadence.

Falwell: He's sort of a Samson figure here.

Robertson: Yes. And now we're in an ape marketplace, and he's tearing it apart.

Falwell: Casting the moneylenders from the temple.

Robertson: Did he just say, "Render unto Dr. Zaius what is Dr. Zaius's," or did I mishear that?

Falwell: I think the meaning is clear, regardless of whether he said it or not.

Robertson: Now we appear to be in some kind of ape museum and there are dioramas with humans posed in various scenes in their natural habitat on this planet.

Falwell: A heretical fantasy unsurprisingly shared by these heretics on this ape planet. We know that cavemen are the stuff of cartoons and pulp novels. It just doesn't match the Scripture.

Robertson: Yeah, not only are the apes mistaken in their religion, but their science also seems to represent the very worst aspects of human science—in this case, the human science that existed 2,000 years before on a distant planet. I wonder whether Jesus has yet returned to Earth at this time?

Falwell: More beatings and humiliation from the gorillas. We could call this movie *The Passion of Charlton Heston*.

Robertson: He's being stoned in the middle of the ape village. The director's laying it on a bit thick, don't you think?

Falwell: I think Heston is maybe at his best when he's suffering biblical torments. "Take your stinking paws off me, you damn dirty ape." I won't forget that line anytime soon.

Robertson: I think he was saying what we all feel.

Falwell: Here he is back in captivity and cavorting with his heathen tribe-girl. I, of course, disapprove of this.

Robertson: Well, they haven't been married.

Falwell: Under the eyes of God? No.

Robertson: But the fact that there are no priests on this planet forgives him somewhat.

Falwell: I don't think you can marry yourself. It does present a bit of a conundrum.

Robertson: I wish Taylor didn't swear so much. He likes to say "damn." A lot.

Falwell: Well, he is in extreme circumstances, but I do agree. If we don't watch our tongue, and obey the Word, we are no better than apes ourselves.

Robertson: Then again, there's a lot to damn in this world, and damnation might not be the wrong feeling, the wrong message, to be sending.

Falwell: This is, verily, a kind of hell. Here come some apes. I don't like the looks of this.

Robertson: Yes, these are the Pharisee guards taking Taylor to the show trial.

Falwell: So it looks like we're at some kind of monkey tribunal. Monkey trials never end well for humans, I must say. We saw it in Scopes, and we're seeing it here too.

Robertson: Yes, it looks like Heston is standing before Herod, Pilate, and Dr. Zaius all at once. Yes, we have an ape theologian as well as their head of science to cast judgment upon Taylor. And, oh, my... Heston is stripped nude once more.

Falwell: In his nudity, he's more noble than the clothed apes. And, of course, the camera angle gives us a kind of cinematic fig leaf.

Robertson: "This exhibit is indeed a man and therefore has no rights under ape law," says the judge. I'm appalled by the sophistry of these arguments. And here we have the ape version of Clarence Darrow.

Falwell: He weaves a web of rhetoric that casts a noxious cloud over the plain and simple logic of the truth and the light.

Robertson: "I am just a simple ape, not used to your sophisticated city ways." Now, the court laughs off Taylor's claim that he has arrived from another planet in a spaceship. Laughing it off—does this remind you of anything? You know, like, perhaps Christ claiming that he's the son of God and being laughed at by the Pharisees?

Falwell: Well, I think it's also true that man doesn't judge man; God judges man. And if that's true, what can we hope and expect from a court of apes?

Robertson: To verify Taylor's claim that he is indeed a man from outer space, they are going to go to one of his captured companions. They've brought the companions out to an amphitheater. Perhaps this will prove Taylor's claim, and everyone will realize that he's not a dumb animal but a thinking, sentient being. He identifies his friend. Speaks to him. There's no response. Landon is his name. Jumpin' Jehosephat!

Falwell: There's a scar on his head.

Robertson: Landon has been lobotomized.

Falwell: Heston's rebelling at his trial. It's the act of a desperate man. I would have liked to see him take a peaceful path, but, as we know from our own nation's experience, sometimes peace is not the answer.

Robertson: And while I loathe his pagan beliefs, Dr. Zaius's administrative abilities are impressive; his sense and his caution— the limitations he places on other apes about what they should and shouldn't know—are commendable. He believes he's protecting them from themselves, and I understand that point of view.

Falwell: We all want to be custodians for what we think is right.

Robertson: Fortunately, we know what's right.

Falwell: Unlike Dr. Zaius. They're talking about missing links in evolutionary chains here. This all just seems like so much monkey business.

Robertson: Dr. Zaius is now telling Taylor that his doom is sealed. He's right about one thing; he says that his fate is preordained. I don't think we could argue with that. Shades of Pilate here. Dr. Zaius is reluctantly doing what he believes is right, what he has to do, but clearly he's confused about the fate he's about to consign Taylor to.

Falwell: And ultimately sinning in the worst way. Here though, the monkeys, the good apes—the ones who are susceptible to the Word—are freeing Heston's character. Heston has changed Zira's and Cornelius's lives. They won't be the same. No one can be the same after you know the truth. Once you hear the Word there's no going back.

Robertson: Amen.

Falwell: It's good to see Charlton Heston with the gun. And you know those apes will only be able to take it from his cold, dead, opposably-digited hands. They've fled back into the Holy Land, from which our Christian hero sprung. Heston is shaving—he's regaining some of his human quality. Uh-oh, but now there's trouble. The gorillas are after our heroes.

Robertson: The apes have tracked them down, deep inside the Holy Land, in front of this cave on the ocean. Heston, unsurprisingly, is showing remarkable marksmanship with his gun. Not surprisingly, he seems to be the only one who really knows how to handle a firearm in this confrontation. Now Dr. Zaius, his group of armed guards having pulled away, is being taken into the cave where Heston, Cornelius, and Dr. Zira are going to look at an archaeological dig that has been conducted by Cornelius. His contention being that there's evidence of a human species that predates this ape society.

Falwell: And it's difficult to figure out. We know, of course, that apes did not prefigure humans in our society. If the movie is trying to say—

Robertson: This all seems beside the point to me. Who really cares?

Falwell: This is a fable of which I can make no sense.

Robertson: I find it really the least compelling part of this movie.

Falwell: They're in the cave now.

Robertson: And there appears to be various levels of the dig. Cornelius has found evidence of an early ape creature. He goes lower and finds even earlier evidence of ape culture, but at the bottom he find various artifacts that seem to be of human origin. And the more ancient culture is more advanced. This, you know... who really cares?

Falwell: Well, if we consider that a culture that is ancient is perhaps closer to God and creation, there is a certain kind of advancement there. We have strayed far.

Robertson: I think that perhaps a territorial claim could be made: We existed here before you did; ergo, we have the right to kick you off the land now and claim this as our own. I could respect that, but, you know, they're talking about thousands of years.

Falwell: We know that archeology can date only 6,000 years. The universe is no older. Bishop Usher said so.

Robertson: Which would be 8,000 years before this time.

Falwell: True. Oh, look, they found a doll... a human doll.

Robertson: Cornelius sensibly asks why a human doll would be made by apes, which Dr. Zaius believes is the only intelligent species that could have created a human doll.

Falwell: Zaius also refers to a scripture and, um—

Robertson: —a lawgiver—

Falwell: Right. While this sounds familiar, it can't be *the* Scripture.

Robertson: You mean the true Scripture. It's a perverted version of the true Scripture. He's somehow been led astray.

Falwell: Zaius is full of it. Forget what I said before. I hope Heston smites him.

Robertson: The human doll talks.

Falwell: That's kind of creepy.

Robertson: Dr. Zaius is certainly going to have to deal with this piece of evidence.

Falwell: Who would make a human doll that talks?

Robertson: Gunfire outside.

Falwell: Trouble's afoot.

Robertson: Heston expertly dispatches a few apes with the rifle.

Falwell: Those apes certainly don't stand a chance against our friend from the NRA.

Robertson: Heston was shooting apes back when these apes were in zoos.

Falwell: Heston has captured Dr. Zaius. He's got him hostage.

Robertson: Now he's requested a horse with food and water.

Falwell: And fifty rounds of ammunition. Good thinking. But I can't help thinking, Pat, if the men on this planet years before were superior, why didn't they survive? And where is the sign of Jesus' presence?

Robertson: They were men forsaken by the Lord, who hadn't heard His Word, or willfully renounced Him. Either way, Taylor comes from the sky to deliver it to them, as Revelation predicts.

Falwell: Perhaps in this earlier human society, feminists and secularists won out. They strayed too far from the path, leaving God no choice but to punish them by enslaving them to monkeys.

Robertson: That's a very good point, Jerry. Who knows what kind of decadent human culture preceded this ape world. Probably one very much like our own.

Falwell: It's a call to action for sure.

Robertson: I don't think it would be too out of line to say that living in a world ruled by apes may very well be the cost of not worshipping the Lord.

Falwell: Praise be—

Robertson: The lot of a godless humanity is to be monkey-slaves.

Falwell: Something funny is going on here—Heston says goodbye to Zira and Cornelius and—no, no, NO, NO! DON'T... NO! Ohhhh. Man-on-ape kissing.

Robertson: Which surely is a precursor to man-on-ape sex. I think we might have to give this one to the censors. And it was so close, so close to being a good Christian story.

Falwell: "Whoever lies with an animal shall surely be put to death." You know from man on ape, there is a logical progression to allowing sodomy, gay marriage. What's next... prostitution? Masturbation?

Robertson: This looks like the end of the movie here. Heston is about to ride off into the sunset with his horse, and I think this is a good time—

Falwell: —with his common-law wife.

Robertson: —with his common-law wife. And I think now is the time when we could summarize what we've learned from this modern Christian parable. This is a story of a man on another planet, surrounded by a tribe of hostile, pagan apes, with nothing but the Word of the Lord to protect him. Dr. Zaius presses Heston on the question of how the world was destroyed and whether it was man's fault. It seems like a race of godless men is very capable of destroying the planet.

Falwell: If we were to assume that the apocalypse that occurred here was born of man, this looks like the Rapture to me—the tribulation in which the only living are sinners who have not accepted the Lord God as their savior and all those unfortunate enough not to have had access to the Word of God.

Robertson: And their offspring.

Falwell: Yes. And their offspring. "What will Taylor find out there?" asks Zira to Dr. Zaius.

Robertson: "His destiny."

Falwell: What could that mean?

Robertson: I don't know. This has to be over. Why aren't the credits rolling?

Falwell: There's some flute music.

Robertson: I don't quite see where this is going. I mean, they're on a beach.

Falwell: They're riding a horse.

Robertson: I really don't see where this is going, Jerry.

Falwell: Me neither, Pat.

Robertson: Okay, we're on the beach.

Falwell: Yawn.

Robertson: Oh, I see something.

Falwell: What is that? It looks like a rusted, corrugated structure.

Robertson: Or some kind of torn wreckage. It looks like it's been underwater. We have some kind of sharp, jagged object here. Looks like a spiky wheel. "Oh, my God. I'm back. I'm home."

Falwell: "They finally really did it. You maniacs." Heston sinks to his knees. "You blew it up. Goddamn you." Those are strong words. "Goddamn you all to hell."

Robertson: What's going on here?

Falwell: Oh, my. It's the Statue of Liberty. It was Earth all along.

Robertson: What does that mean? I hate to say I told you so, but... this just lends credence to what we were speaking of before.

Falwell: That the apes blew up the Statue of Liberty?

Robertson: No, that humans blew up the Statue of Liberty, that godless, lesbian, decadent—

Falwell: —feminists and the ACLU! We've seen it before, and here we've seen it carried out to its logical, if devastating, conclusion. Lower Manhattan, itself somewhat of a godless land, is destined to be destroyed by the degradations of our own society.

Robertson: Yes, how fitting that the symbol of the apocalypse would be the Statue of Liberty, that symbol of New York, our own Sodom and Gomorrah.

Falwell: What I can't figure out is, where's the rebirth in all of this? Where's the message of hope? Because any movie that truly serves God must have a message of hope in there somewhere.

Robertson: You're right. Maybe this isn't a Christian movie at all.

STAR WARS: EPISODE I—
THE PHANTOM MENACE

[RNC FEATURED-MERCHANDISE DVD]

Commentary by Dick Cheney and William Bennett

Recorded July 2003

WILLIAM BENNETT: Do you remember the first time you heard about the whole *Star Wars* phenomenon?

DICK CHENEY: Yeah, I was in D.C. at the time, running for the Wyoming House seat. Lines of people were wrapped around the block waiting to see this movie.

Bennett: Yeah, that was 1971? '74?

Cheney: No, it was definitely after Nixon was out of office.

Bennett: Was this a Jerry Ford-era film?

Cheney: I think Ford. Or maybe early Carter. It was ages ago.

Bennett: I remember there was a lot of to-do about this movie. My kids were very excited about it. I think they must have seen it four or five times. That, and *The E.T.* Do you remember *The E.T.*?

Cheney: Yeah, *E.T.* That was great.

Bennett: It was a profoundly moral film.

Cheney: Sure, Bill. *Episode I.* This makes sense. This is the first movie. *The Phantom Menace.*

Bennett: So, this was '78.

Cheney: Yeah, something like that.

Bennett: "Turmoil has engulfed the Galactic Republic. The taxation…" Taxation!?!

Cheney: Very interesting. "The taxation of trade routes to outlying star systems is in dispute." I had no idea this movie was so interested in trade and tax issues.

Bennett: It seems some sort of blockade has been set up by the Trade Federation to stop shipping to a small planet called Naboo.

Cheney: Huh. Naboo. "While the congress of the Republic endlessly debate—" We know what that's like.

Bennett: "—endlessly debates this alarming chain of events, the Supreme Chancellor has secretly dispatched two Jedi knights, the guardians of peace and justice." I can't read the rest. It disappeared.

Cheney: It's really hard to read it.

Bennett: Why did they do it this way?

Cheney: I don't know. It keeps running away from me. We have a spaceship flying.

Bennett: So this takes place in the future, this film.

Cheney: Yes, the future.

Bennett: 1978? *Star Wars*!

Cheney: Right! *Star Wars*. This was what Reagan was talking about. This was where we got the name for the missile defense shield program.

Bennett: This film was his idea, if I'm not mistaken.

Cheney: I think you are mistaken. But I think he based the system on this movie and, really, these are astonishing special effects.

Bennett: It looks awfully good for a movie made in the late seventies. Now we have two men in robes arriving at Naboo here. Is this where they are? With robots?

Cheney: I guess it could be. Naboo is a big spaceship?

Bennett: And the robots and the robed men are talking. Is this the Trade Federation? What's happening here?

Cheney: That's a good question. It looks like the Tin Man from *The Wizard of Oz*.

Bennett: But it's a tin woman.

Cheney: Tin woman. And two monks.

Bennett: I think one of those men... is that actor Liam Neeson?

Cheney: Yes, that's Liam Neeson. The short one. I mean... the tall one.

Bennett: But he would have been a young man in 1968. Right?

Cheney: Late seventies, Bill. Must be makeup.

Bennett: The profound moral lesson of the *Star Wars* films is, as far as I understand them, about "resisting the dark side of the force"—that's how people refer to it.

Cheney: Yeah, T-shirts used to say that.

Bennett: And so the Darth Vader we'll see in this movie... I assume we'll meet him. And we'll meet—what is his name?

Cheney: There's Duke Skywalker.

Bennett: Yes. Or is it Lance? I thought it was Lance. I think the shorter man with Neeson taking tea from the Tin Man is Lance.

Cheney: I thought this movie was much more exciting. I mean, all we've seen is something about taxation and men drinking tea.

Bennett: We have a holographic evil man talking to fishmen about something.

Cheney: I think I'm just going to have sit back and watch this for awhile and try to take in what's going on here. I'm very confused.

Bennett: Who has the missile defense technology and who is frustrating its completion? Who is attempting to make it work and who are the people impeding the progress of missile defense?

Cheney: That remains to be seen.

Bennett: Well, these two people who came with the monks have just exploded. They've been killed. I'm going to have to tick the "Violence" box on my morality checklist.

Cheney: They're holding swords made out of light.

Bennett: The light-swords. So they're fighting a bunch of robots of some kind with their light-swords. Now, they're in charge of solving this dispute, and they're doing so with their light-swords, and the fishmen are frightened of them. One is often forced to use force to dissuade evil robots who want to enslave the galaxy with unfair trade and Draconian taxation laws.

Cheney: Well, the real problem here is that the Chinese fish-men—and there's something weirdly Chinese about these guys—don't seem to have enough force to back them up. Two men with light-swords are basically tearing apart their entire ship.

Bennett: But look! The Jedi are frightened of the rolling force-field robots.

Cheney: Yeah, these have shields.

Bennett: Aha! And the Jedi run away, proving that shields are inherently terrifying. Did you hear? They just mentioned "Naboo." Liam Neeson said, "We have to warn Chancellor Valorum about Naboo." So this isn't Naboo.

Cheney: Where's Liam Neeson's character from? His name sounds Chinese to me.

Bennett: His name is Qui-Gon Jinn. I've written it down here.

Cheney: It sounds Chinese. And this woman looks Chinese, too. She looks like a dowager empress from the nineteenth century.

Bennett: The queen that the fishmen are talking to?

Cheney: Yeah.

Bennett: She's the queen from Naboo.

Cheney: Still looks Chinese to me.

Bennett: She does. What is going on here?

Cheney: I don't know. I'm having a very hard time sorting it out.

Bennett: Is this movie a piece of Chinese glorification? That would trouble me profoundly.

Cheney: It's some kind of futuristic Chinese parable with talking fish and Chinese emperors.

Bennett: So everyone's Chinese!

Cheney: So far. The two men that blew up in the spaceship didn't look Chinese.

Bennett: Now, here, another holographic man is talking to the Nabooians. The Naboans? What would they be called?

Cheney: The Nabooites?

Bennett: He's a senator named Palpatine. This transmission's being jammed by the greedy Trade Federation, and everyone seems to think that invasion is in the imminent here.

Cheney: I'm so confused! She's a princess, and this is her council.

Bennett: Yes.

Cheney: Is this a constitutional monarchy?

Bennett: That's a good question.

Cheney: Or is it a just a regular, plain old monarchy? I don't see a parliament that's being consulted here. But yet she's part of a larger, intergalactic parliament.

Bennett: Yes, she's in the Intergalactic Senate, and that's how they resolve things in this system insofar as I can understand. And this system sends out these Jedi-knight-monk-people to solve disputes. And they use their light-swords, except when robots with shields appear. With anything that has shields, you just have to flee instantly.

Cheney: Yeah, shields are definitely the key to military power, as far as I can see. Oh, here are the armies of the Trade Federation.

Bennett: The greedy Chinese fishman Trade Federation is landing on the planet. Liam Neeson is tackled by some weird animal.

Cheney: I have to say, the popularity of the film mystifies me.

Bennett: I'm not really understanding it. The morality of the film seems much more opaque than I'm comfortable with.

Cheney: But it's hard to find a clear-cut morality about tax issues.

Bennett: Yeah, unless the greedy, Chinese fishmen are forcing it on the rest of the galaxy. Then you just have to cut them up with your light-swords. In that case, the moral seems really clear.

Cheney: We're underwater now.

Bennett: A very beautiful, glowing city that this stuttering animal claims to live in.

Cheney: His name is Jar Jar.

Bennett: Jar JAR?

Cheney: Jar Jar Binks.

Bennett: Does he have a speech impediment? Is it just Jar Binks?

Cheney: That's unclear. I'm finding it very hard to believe that these idiot creatures built such a tremendous underwater city.

Bennett: Jar Binks and his people?

Cheney: Yeah. They don't seem very bright to me.

Bennett: And here are Liam Neeson and Lance Skywalker making friends with frog and camel people they've discovered underwater.

Cheney: They seem to be crafty about making allies.

Bennett: You know, Kissinger said it best: "He's a bastard, but he's our bastard." In Liam Neeson's case, he's probably thinking, "He's a funny-talking fat frog, but he's my funny-talking fat frog." Right? Again, the special effects here as the ship leaves the underwater city—I'm very impressed.

Cheney: Are you sure this is from the late seventies?

Bennett: I'm fairly sure, because I remember, you know, the *Star Wars* phenomenon was part of a general cultural and moral trend. I don't know… it's disco, cocaine, key parties, fondue—you know, that whole scene.

Cheney: I remember.

Bennett: I associate them all together. But this has to be the first film. It has "Episode I" written right on it.

Cheney: Right.

Bennett: George Lucas made this film, didn't he?

Cheney: Yeah, George Lucas did.

Bennett: *American Graffiti*, too. What a wonderful film that was.

Cheney: It was a good film.

Cheney: Wait, another giant fish? Didn't we already have them get attacked by a sea monster?

Bennett: Well, they're in the middle of the planet core—

Cheney: It just seems kind of played out.

Bennett: What? That they've been attacked by five sea monsters?

Cheney: Yeah.

Bennett: Yeah, well, you know.

Cheney: Did you like that… "played out"? I picked that up from my daughter.

Bennett: Your daughter must have really liked these films. She was a young woman when they came out.

Cheney: She loved a character called Princess Leia and a talking robot. She was really into a Princess Leia.

Bennett: So maybe that's the Chinese princess we've seen.

Cheney: It's possible. I haven't caught any names yet.

Bennett: Well, so far we've got Palpatine, Liam Neeson or "Qui-Gon Jinn," Lance Skywalker, and Jar Binks.

Cheney: We see this gigantic army marching toward the Naboo city. Do you mean to tell me that they don't have a nuke that they can just drop on these people?

Bennett: There's not a lot of bombing that goes on here, is there?

Cheney: It's very strange. You'd think that since war—modern war, at least—is strategically based upon air strikes and artillery, you would see it here, initially at least.

Bennett: Right. So maybe the Chinese fishmen just want to capture Princess Leia.

Cheney: Perhaps. But what about the Nabooites? Why aren't they defending themselves?

Bennett: Look at them. They're a bunch of helpless, welfare-state, European pansies who like their vacations long and their architecture fancy. These people don't know how to fight for freedom.

Cheney: The queen looks like a Kabuki actress now.

Bennett: Princess Leia?

Cheney: Yeah.

Bennett: She's wearing some black feather, too. She looks like an ostrich.

Cheney: That's really strange. I'm getting lost.

Bennett: Did they build these robots especially for this movie?

Cheney: I don't know. This is extremely bizarre, because I feel like I'm looking at the robots from the future standing next to Italians from the Renaissance.

Bennett: Yeah. Meanwhile, Princess Leia seems just as puzzled as we are by this. And it looks like Earth Wind & Fire is in her entourage. Liam Neeson and Lance Skywalker are going to take care of this, it looks like. Thank goodness. Maybe they'll explain what's going on.

Cheney: I hope so.

Bennett: Who are the greedy, taxing Trade Federation guys? Those are the Chinese fishmen.

Cheney: I'm a little skeptical. I mean, we haven't really gotten both sides of the story here about the taxation issue. Taxes are a very complicated issue. They don't reduce well to movie plots.

Bennett: What did the black pilot they just liberated explain to Liam Neeson?

Cheney: He said the fishmen want her to sign a treaty to make their invasion legal.

Bennett: Yes, that sounds very familiar.

Cheney: Good strategy.

Bennett: Now they're escaping this planet and their ship is under attack. Obviously, Liam Neeson does not have shield technology. You see? The trash-can robot has put a shield on the ship, and it got away. This whole universe is based on shield technology.

Cheney: He who has the shield controls this universe.

Bennett: Why are there people who want to impeach shield technology? It's mind-boggling, isn't it? And there are people who want to keep us shieldless in a dangerous world. Do you think the Chinese fishmen are going to pause for developing shields?

Cheney: I think they're already well along their way to having shields. And, if for no other reason than that, the Nabooians need to create shields of their own.

Bennett: They need to create guns, too, from the look of it. They don't even have that. A bunch of robots took their entire planet over in less than a day! They make the Afghani people look like Russians in Stalingrad, for God's sake.

Cheney: Wait... there's a man with incredible makeup on his face.

Bennett: He's with Senator Palpatine, talking to the Chinese fish-men. They're talking about these two men like they should have known about this. "We shouldn't have made this bargain." I have to ask again: What's going on? What are they talking about?

Cheney: I have no clue. How many different parties do we have here? We've got Chinese fishmen. We've got two separate people in robes, but they don't seem to be on the same side. And then we've got the trash-can robots. We've got underwater, retarded creatures. We've got Earth Wind & Fire. I don't know what to make of this.

Bennett: I think the universe is a confused place.

Cheney: This movie was definitely made in the sixties or seventies. Lance Skywalker has a ponytail.

Bennett: Oh, yes... he does.

Cheney: There's kind of a hippie thing going on. It's the fashion of the times.

Bennett: Now they're on a desert planet. The *whole* planet is a desert?

Cheney: Presumably.

Bennett: And they're going to find shields.

Cheney: Interesting.

Bennett: Her Highness, Princess Leia, is asking Liam Neeson to take her handmaiden with her, who is the same person.

Cheney: The same person as who?

Bennett: As Princess Leia. They look exactly the same. And they have a trash can following them.

Cheney: I'm going to have to take this all in.

Bennett: Are you okay? You look very confused.

Cheney: I am very confused. I don't like to be this confused. I should have had someone brief me on this before we started.

Bennett: Yeah, some talking points would have really helped. I've written down several things here, and it's mostly just amounted to, well, I've written "shield" seven times here. That's all I've written. Now they are in some sort of desert city. It looks like a... I would say it's a Muslim city. Wouldn't you?

Cheney: It looks like a Muslim city.

Bennett: But with a lot more gigantic lizards wearing saddles.

Cheney: Wait... subtitles.

Bennett: The Nubians? They're looking for Nubians. This makes it a slightly different movie.

Cheney: Maybe this isn't a Muslim city.

Bennett: They're looking for a spare part for their spaceship, and they're in a shop with a flying blue creature and a cute little kid.

Cheney: You know, this is some terrible acting here. This little kid is really awful. Bill, I think I'm about ready to throw in the towel. I don't care what Rove says about the 18-to-24-year-old demographic, this movie is cowshit. Taxation, retarded creatures—

Bennett: Hold on! So the boy just said that he was lost because there was some betting going on, some gambling. Where is the gambling? What are they betting on?

Cheney: I don't know. He said something about a pod race.

Bennett: Well that sounds interesting.

Cheney: Sure does, Bill.

Bennett: It's almost as exciting as shields. I'm going to have to write "pod racing" down here on my talking points.

Cheney: I just can't get over how terrible that kid is.

Bennett: Yeah. I don't like him either. But children play an important role in moral stories. Did he just say, "Yippee!"?

Cheney: He still looks pretty tough, Bill.

Bennett: Heavens to Betsy! I hope we get to see some of that pod racing. Sebulba looks like he'd be a fierce competitor.

Cheney: You favor Sebulba?

Bennett: I put $20 on Sebulba.

Cheney: Oh, get serious, Bill.

Bennett: I'm serious.

Cheney: Place some real stakes here.

Bennett: $50 on Sebulba! I think he's going to take that pod race.

Cheney: Oh, come on, Bill. Make it worth my while. If I'm going to sit through this piece of crap—

Bennett: $500 Sebulba beats that kid in this pod race.

Cheney: $5,000 and you've got a bet.

Bennett: We have a bet. $5,000 Sebulba wins it.

Cheney: All right. I'm gonna go for the kid, I think.

Bennett: You're going to take the kid?!?

Cheney: Yeah, I'm gonna take the kid. You in for twenty?

Bennett: You were just telling me you didn't like the kid.

Cheney: I don't like the kid, but I like his chances in the pod race.

Bennett: I don't understand. Let's just say you're a little out of your league here, Dick.

Cheney: You're right. I wouldn't compare my gambling skills to yours. You have an instinct for it. Are you in?

Bennett: Definitely. Can I admit something to you?

Cheney: Sure.

Bennett: Other than the shield-based technology, which is obviously the wonderful thing about this movie, I was about ready to give up on it until they started talking about the pod racing.

Cheney: Well, I'm definitely in it through the pod race now so I can get my $20,000.

Bennett: Looks here like the slaves have their own quarters.

Cheney: It's a pretty nice slave house.

Bennett: Now we're to understand that the little boy invented this robot, which seems to me to be, shall we say, a bit effeminate. What are the programming benefits of an effeminate robot?

Cheney: This thing may be only a bit less annoying than the boy.

Bennett: Yeah. I have to wonder, what is the benefit of giving robots emotions? Wouldn't you want to make them as emotionless as possible? Otherwise you just have to deal with all of this baggage, all this whining. I mean, say this robot likes the pod racing. And you find the robot down at the pod-racing track. It sees you there. There's an awkward moment. You have to deal with that. Maybe the robot tells your wife that he saw you at the pod races. You see the difficulties of the robot that has feelings and wants of its own. Frankly, I think it's a Pandora's box.

Cheney: He seems kind of insecure, too, that robot. He's not like the other robots.

Bennett: There are a lot of robots. There are just as many robots as people. Look at this? Where are we now? A gigantic city planet that we're on? And there are the two black-robed men. That's the senator we've seen too much of.

Cheney: Oh, there's the one with the face, with the tattoos.

Bennett: No, he's the devil from the Red Hots box.

Cheney: He must be a bad guy.

Bennett: Maybe that's Darth Vader.

Cheney: They did say, "Darth," didn't they?

Bennett: They called him Darth something.

Cheney: Yeah, Darth Vader.

Bennett: Are you wishing that something bad would happen to Jar Binks? Like, maybe he'll be killed in the pod racing?

Cheney: If we're lucky.

Bennett: I'll give you $50 if that happens.

Cheney: $50? That's all you're gonna do?

Bennett: Okay, $2,000 if Jar Binks gets killed in the pod racing.

Cheney: I don't know. I think maybe if you up that to $20,000, I'll take you. C'mon, Bill, you just sold another *Book of Virtues*.

Bennett: I know. I've had a lot of heat on me right now with the slot-machine business. Is it okay for me to be saying this?

Cheney: I think so, yeah. We can edit this stuff out. FOX is doing it. We can trust FOX.

Bennett: Oh, why didn't you just say so! I'll give you thirty-five.

Cheney: All right. $35,000.

Bennett: So I have fifty-five riding on this pod race?

Cheney: Yeah, $55,000.

Bennett: That's not too bad. I'm pretty excited about this. So, after talking it over, they've decided that their only way off the planet is to sponsor a boy in a pod race whose master will then trade a part of a ship that they don't have money to pay for.

Cheney: Sounds like a really sensible plan. Or they could fly their spaceship over this town, point their lasers at it and say, "Give us the thing, or we blow you up."

Bennett: Maybe intergalactic space law prohibits that kind of action. Liam Neeson's putting up his ship as the entry fee.

Cheney: That, I would say, is reckless gambling, Bill. I think you might even agree with me.

Bennett: Yeah, I only did that once. And I got very lucky, I have to say. They're talking a lot about gambling here in this scene. This is the winged blue man and Liam Neeson and they're making the bet more complicated.

Cheney: They're talking pods, and they're adding higher stakes.

Bennett: As much as I enjoy this, why doesn't Liam Neeson just take out his light-sword and singe one of the blue guy's wings right off? And say, "Look, you're gonna give me that part, and you're gonna like it." Is that immoral? This guy is a slaver! Liam Neeson was just telling Lance Skywalker that there's something special about this boy, the boy that you think is going to take Sebulba in the pod race. Sebulba is obviously the meanest pod racer in this whole godforsaken backwater. Why did you make that bet?

Cheney: I don't know. I'm feeling lucky.

Bennett: I understand. These "Jedi mind tricks" are fine, but when you get down to it, in a pod race it's all about who's the most ruthless and who wants it the most. Do you think that kid wants it?

Cheney: Yeah, I don't know if that kid's really had enough life experience to want a pod race.

Bennett: Sebulba wears his life on his reptilian face. This is a guy that will kill you for throwing a chicken at him. This guy in a pod race is not someone you want to bet against. I'm sorry. I know it's a movie. We're having a good time. But you are out of your depth.

Cheney: Is this mother about to give her annoying child up to a complete stranger? This kid is just awful.

Bennett: I think so. And I think she just claimed he was an immaculate conception.

Cheney: An immaculate conception?

Bennett: Yeah.

Cheney: Whatever helps you get to sleep at night.

Bennett: It's a strange movie.

Cheney: I still can't imagine people lining up around the block to see this movie a second time.

Bennett: I can't either. It doesn't make any sense the first time. I have to say that the little boy's pod that we're getting a look at for the first time is quite impressive. It works, for one, which is surprising to me. I'm not worried. My money is pretty safe. You see this little kid. He's surrounded by a bunch of reprobates. They're obviously all slaves. I have respect for these slaves and the situation they're in. It's terrible, et cetera, et cetera. But, when you get down to it, Sebulba is going to destroy them.

Cheney: Do you always gloat like this, Bill, before a race?

Bennett: Am I gloating? I wasn't even aware I was just talking actually. The Red Hot devil is now visiting the desert planet. He's sending out some more robots, some different robots.

Cheney: Again with the Red Hots. I didn't know you were such a candy fan, Bill.

Bennett: They sell them at Foxwoods. They keep me awake. There's Sebulba. There's my boy. Two blue-haired women in coveralls are massaging him. He's knows what he's doing. And here Annie's preparing for his race. We've got Princess Leia there, and the little boy, he's never won a race. Sebulba has very flashy, Amelia Earhart-style aviator goggles. Where do you think they filmed this pod-racing sequence?

Cheney: It looks like it could be in Arizona. And there's the mother's love. That's why the kid is going to win.

Bennett: Sebulba's sabotaging the kid's ship!

Cheney: Wait a minute! That's not fair.

Bennett: I'm sorry. You're the one who made the bet, Dick. I'm sorry. You know, I think Sebulba is just playing tough. He's a competitor. He knows what he's doing. This is going to be an exciting race. Hey, wait a minute. Is Liam Neeson giving the kid some advice?

Cheney: He's allowed to give the kid some advice.

Bennett: He's saying concentrate on the moment and live in the... What is he's saying? That seemed like it could have been insider information.

Cheney: You already made the bet, man.

Bennett: Alright! The race is about to start. I think your boy is easily the youngest person in this race.

Cheney: He also appears to be the only human.

Bennett: Wait a minute. Does that give him an unfair advantage?

Cheney: I don't know.

Bennett: Well, as the race gets underway, it looks like your boy's pod racer is stalled out.

Cheney: Yeah, thanks to the sabotage of your man.

Bennett: I think the announcer just called him "Anakin Skywalker." Is that possible?

Cheney: Anything is possible at this point.

Bennett: Do you see Sebulba call that guy a "slimo" and slam him into the canyon wall? I think you made a bad bet, Dick. I do have one question, though, as much as I'm enjoying the pod racing: What kind of mother lets her son engage in this type of activity?

Cheney: Can you imagine living with this kid? It makes sense.

Bennett: First lap is over. Sebulba is in first place. How do you feel about that, Dick?

Cheney: Two more laps.

Bennett: It's a shame about the racer whose engine was destroyed by his own pit crew being sucked into it. I'm glad I didn't bet on him. We see the little boy having some more problems here. His engine has come unattached to his pod, and frankly I'm just enjoying this whole sequence here. He's a clever little tyke, though, isn't he? He can fix any problem that comes up. But I still feel very good about Sebulba. I think Sebulba has it well in hand, here. His ship is much bigger. He's much more experienced. He's won several times. Shit! Somehow he's lost the lead!

Cheney: Yes!

Bennett: So Skywalker is now in the lead. Again, I'm not terribly concerned. I think Sebulba's just—

Cheney: Come on, Skywalker! Come on, Skywalker!

Bennett: Sebulba is probably letting this happen. Now here we see the sabotage Sebulba engineered earlier coming to the fore. It's working exactly as he planned. Skywalker's engine is on fire. Sebulba is in the lead! How is Skywalker driving what look to be 700 miles an hour and fixing his engine? He's eight years old.

Cheney: He's a terrible actor but a great pod racer. That's all I have to say.

Bennett: That is a lot of ground to make up. I think Sebulba's going to be okay. I definitely think he's going to be okay. What do we have riding on this? I bet you, what, $700?

Cheney: No, I think it was a bit more than $700.

Bennett: Can we stop this? I think—

Cheney: No, no. Come on, Bill, here we go, the final stretch.

Bennett: Where's my assistant? She's, uh, I'm being paged.

Cheney: Sit down, Bill. Come on, Skywalker!

Bennett: Frankly, there's no proof that I ever took that bet.

Cheney: Oh, we've got the bet on tape. Don't be a liar too, Bill.

Bennett: I'm not a liar. I'm just saying—

Cheney: Sebulba and Skywalker are neck and neck—

Bennett and Cheney: OH!

Cheney: What happened?

Bennett: Sebulba's pod is destroyed.

Cheney: Yes!

Bennett: "Whodoo" is what he says. I have to agree with him, frankly. What is this movie about, again? Is there a greedy Trade Federation to divert my attention from my economic ruin?

Cheney: Watch the movie, Bill.

Bennett: Double or nothing the Trade Federation wins in the end.

Cheney: I'll take that bet. Double or nothing.

Bennett: So the kid won. I think I need to write another book.

Cheney: Here the flying blue creature is accusing Liam Neeson of having cheated. Liam Neeson certainly seems fairly ruthless as he is squeezing the flying blue man for everything he's worth, doesn't he? Quite the hero.

Bennett: Took quite the risk betting on the kid, though. What would have happened had he lost the bet?

Cheney: I don't know. It seems pretty reckless. I mean, they got Princess Leia, whom they're trying to shield from the evil Trade Federation, and these two guys in cloaks and the Red Hot devil and their Red Hot stuff.

Bennett: Speaking of, here is the Red Hot devil and Liam Neeson fighting with their light-swords.

Cheney: I notice a lack of shield protection for both of them.

Bennett: Exactly. Neither one of them has one and what are we seeing? They are fighting to a stalemate.

Cheney: That would be a crucial edge, I think, if one of them had a shield.

Bennett: True, but nothing can be done about that now. We can only hope that Liam Neeson is working on developing a shield. And now, back on Naboo, the Chinese fishmen are pushing around the Nabooians while sitting in these chairs that walk by themselves. That's the decadence of their Chinese fishman rule. This universe seems driven by their greedy, corrupt insistence on unfairly taxing the people.

Cheney: There does seem to be a problem with taxation. Taxes might be too high for everybody in this galaxy.

Bennett: Here we have a ship cruising into the planet Coruscant; this is one of the talking notes my assistant gave me. "Coruscant. The entire planet is one big city," the pilot says. Apparently he's Captain Narration. Again, the popularity of *Star Wars* films is certainly a little suspect at this point.

Cheney: Although, the special effects continue to surprise me.

Bennett: They're amazing. Amazing! For 1970s technology, this movie is incredible. Princess Leia is wearing the black ostrich outfit again. I think here we're going to get some insight into the parliamentary and governmental policies on Coruscant. And there's Chancellor Valorum. He is the head of the Federation. He's called a special session of the senate. They're going to address the invasion of Naboo by the greedy Trade Federation. I'm very excited. This is starting to get a little bit more actively and directly involved into our world.

Cheney: This could be interesting. This could be very interesting. It'll be interesting to see what kind of parliamentary procedures will be employed. What are much less compelling are these hints of some kind of romantic involvement between this tyke and the princess.

Bennett: Yeah. Here Senator Palpatine is telling Princess Leia—

Cheney: Who has a kind of white dreadlock thing going on now.

Bennett: Now, the reason the Republic doesn't work, according to the evil, duplicitous Senator Palpatine, is that it's all politics. There's no vision. What do you have to say about that?

Cheney: I'm a little bit more interested in this council of strange alien creatures that are talking in another room.

Bennett: Look how unusual they are! There's a small green one. And one with a pointy head. And then a bald, black one. Very exotic. These are the Jedis, right? We've heard about how they wield the force. They have shield technology.

Cheney: They definitely have shield technology.

Bennett: Apparently the boy is the one who will bring balance to the force. That is what they're discussing now.

Cheney: What's the force?

Bennett: The force is what controls the dice when you roll them. It controls whether or not you get a five or a seven if you're showing fifteen.

Cheney: Sounds like a lot of mumbo jumbo to me, I have to say.

Bennett: I think everyone acknowledges that some force has some rule in our lives. So here we get out first glimpse of the Federation Senate, the galactic senate. It seems like they have maybe a few too many delegates.

Cheney: This looks like chaos, really. I can't imagine a debate.

Bennett: There are, I'm going to say, 5,000 delegates.

Cheney: How many parties do you think there are?

Bennett: I don't know. And anyone apparently can just talk at any moment. Valorum is not really controlling things in here very well at all.

Cheney: Yeah, it is a little messed up. Those are very neat little floating desks.

Bennett: What easy work it would be for an assassin just to sabotage one of these floating disks and wipe out the entire planet's delegation. Do you think there's some sort of security apparatus to monitor the hovering mechanisms of these?

Cheney: Wait, now the fishpeople are talking.

Bennett: Oh, look at this. Somebody is concurring with the Trade Federation about sending a delegation of observers.

Cheney: Bill, how much do you want to bet that this Senator Valorum loses his seat?

Bennett: I'll give you $250 on that.

Cheney: $500.

Bennett: That's a bet.

Cheney: Alright.

Bennett: Here Skywalker is complaining to Liam Neeson that the boy is not going to pass the test. What do you think?

Cheney: I really don't care.

Bennett: $20?

Cheney: I think he's going to pass the test.

Bennett: Apparently we learn here that Senator Palpatine has taken Chancellor Valorum's seat.

Cheney: Two for two.

Bennett: All right. Here, take it. You can count it. It's all there. What do you make of the politics of this universe? Dick, you look a little comatose. You look as though this movie has—

Cheney: I'm bored to tears, I have to tell you. This is the worst movie I have ever seen. It's just terrible.

Bennett: It's not that bad. It had that great pod race.

Cheney: If I hadn't won money off of you watching this movie I'd think this was the biggest waste of time in my life. This is the stupidest idea I've ever heard. Those idiots at the RNC... No demographic is worth this. "It'll be cool to the young voters!" "What else does a vice president do?" Not watch this shit, I'll tell you! Bill, I've got to get out of here. There's a fund-raiser I've got to get to. Jesus, what a load of crap! I don't know how long my heart's gonna keep tickin', and I don't want to die with the voice of that little crappy-actin' prick in my ear when my arms go numb. I'm out of here.

Bennett: How can you say that? There was a terrifically exciting pod race. There's been some interesting talk about trade.

Cheney: This is why you don't learn. You know, you lose money watching the pod race, and you still want to watch pod races.

Bennett: Well, this movie expounds a clear moral vision about how having shields is really important.

Cheney: Sure, there seems to be some value in speaking in very affected accents that change from scene to scene, abandoning your mother to slavery, and teaming up with retarded sea creatures.

Bennett: I don't know why you're so upset. I'm having a good time. How about we make a bet that we can watch this movie to the end?

Cheney: You're on.

ACKNOWLEDGMENTS

Thanks to Lee Epstein (whose book this is too), Amber Hoover (who laughed at this idea's first, timid attempt), Nick Poppy (for brilliant pinch-hitting), and the good people at Blockbuster Video and Video Edge in Park Slope. Special thanks to Laurie Sims, Owen Otto, Amanda Fazzone, Jessica Tonnies, Dustin Perkins, Brian McMullen, David Horowitz, and Alvaro Villanueva, who are all now owed forever. Thanks, too, to all the men and women of Brooklyn's own Special Reserves, without whom this book would not have been possible.

AUTHORS

Tom Bissell is the author of *Chasing the Sea*, a slightly more substantial book, and now lives in a deluxe apartment in the sky in lovely lower Manhattan. He and Jeff Alexander still stay in touch.

Jeff Alexander lives a modest life in his studio apartment on a quiet street in Brooklyn, where he is perfectly content.